THE BLUE SALT ROAD

THE BLUE SALT ROAD

Joanne M. Harris

Illustrated by Bonnie Hawkins

GOLLANCZ

LONDON

First published in Great Britain in 2018 by Gollancz
an imprint of the Orion Publishing Group Ltd
Carmelite House, 50 Victoria Embankment
London EC4Y 0DZ

An Hachette UK Company

1 3 5 7 9 10 8 6 4 2

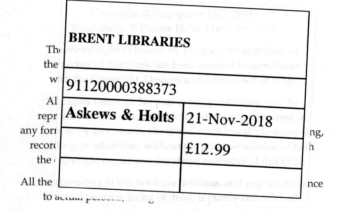
A CIP catalogue record for this book is
available from the British Library.

ISBN (Hardback) 978 1 473 22221 2
ISBN (eBook) 978 1 473 22223 6

Printed and bound in Great Britain by Clays Ltd, Elcograf S.p.A.

MIX
Paper from
responsible sources
FSC® C104740

www.joanne-harris.co.uk
www.gollancz.co.uk

Prologue

The ocean has many voices. It sings in the voice of the pilot whale; the voice of the dolphin; the waves on the beach. It sings in the voice of a thousand birds; it cries in the wind that howls through the rocks upon the distant skerries. But most of all, it sings in the voice of the selkie; those people of the ocean clans that hunt with the seal, and dance with the waves, and, nameless, go on forever.

The voice of the selkie is soft and low. At first you may not hear it. At first you may mistake it for the cry of a bird, or the bark of a seal, or the sound of the tide on the pebbles. But listen, and you will realize that each of those sounds is a story. The crunch of pebbles underfoot; the splash of a leaping mackerel; the cry of a sea-eagle hunting above the white rocky shores of the islands. Stories, like the travelling folk, never die, but always move on. There are stories everywhere; in the air; the food you eat; in the embers of the fire. And when you go to bed at night, and listen to the wind in the eaves, there are stories under the bed and hiding in the shadows. Stories of the Kraken, who comes from the deepest oceans; stories of sirens whose song can lure unwary travellers to their death; stories of mermaids, lighthouses, ships – and stories of the selkie.

This is such a story. Taken from a song of the Folk, taught to me by a gunnerman; which makes it just as true – or false – as those sweet siren promises. The Folk have a complex relationship with the clan of the selkie: hunting them for their hides and flesh; fearing them for their savagery. And yet they have always dreamed of them from the safety of their homes; and, loving them for their wildness, have always sought to capture and tame the people of the ocean. Thus are they both sickened and drawn; bewitched and repelled; at war and in love. They weave their stories from the thinnest and most fragile of threads, thistledown by moonlight; like gleaming skeins of spider silk. This is such a story, as true or as false as the sound of the wind, or the flight of the herring-gull over the white-crested waves. This is *my* story; the story of the land-folk and the seal-folk, a story of love, and of treachery, and of the call of the ocean. Take from it what you most need, and pass it on to someone else, for this is how stories – and selkie – move on; changing, unchanging, like the tides, taking with them what they can and scattering tales to the four winds, like seeds upon the ocean.

Part 1

≈

An earthly nourris sits and sings
And aye she sings, "Ba lilly wean,
Little ken I my bairn's father,
Far less the land that he staps in"

Child Ballad, no. 113

One

There was a young man of the Grey Seal clan, the most playful of the selkie. He lived by a circle of skerries to the west of the islands of the Folk, where the winds blow harsh and, every year, the ice creeps ever closer. His people were fierce and wild and razor-toothed; and he was the wildest of them all, diving from the tallest rocks, tumbling in the whitest surf, roaming further than any of his people dared venture.

His mother was the matriarch of the clan: proud and powerful and strong, sheathed in muscle and robed in fat to keep her through the winters, and her son was just as handsome; with powerful shoulders, dappled flanks and eyes as dark as the ocean.

But the young man was wilful. He loved to listen to tales of the Folk; those people so like, yet so unlike the selkie. He loved to swim close to their shores, and play in the surf of their beaches. He loved to follow their fishing-boats and watch them take in their catches of fish. And he loved to hear their voices, singing from the decks of their ships; voices that reached him on the wind in snippets and snatches of story.

His mother said: "Beware the Folk. Their race is bloodthirsty and cruel. They do not shed their skins, as we do, to walk upon the land, but hunt the grey seal and the walrus with spears and harpoons, and flay their skins, and wear them against the winter cold, for they are thin, pale, shivering things, helpless as new-born chicks in the snow."

But the young man of the selkie did not heed her warnings. Nor did he heed the words of his friends, the carefree companions of his childhood. He knew of the wars between the clans of the selkie and that of the Folk. He had even watched from afar as the whaling-ships set off out from the coast, hunting the regal lords of the sea. He had seen bloody battles fought among the outermost skerries, and he knew of the courage of the Folk, and longed to know more of their customs. And so he swam out to the nearest of the neighbouring islands, and set out to learn everything he could about its mysterious inhabitants.

He would swim close to their homesteads, and

watch the light from their windows, and bask in the shallows by their shores, and listen to their women singing lullabies to their children. He would sit out alone on a rock by the harbour mouth, and watch the tall ships. And as he grew, so grew his desire for the land and its people, until one summer's night he swam right to the shore of an island, and, beaching himself on the cool dark sand, he shed his bulky sealskin, with its protective layer of fat, and stood naked on the shoreline; dark-skinned, sleek and glossy-haired, and handsome in the moonlight.

"So this is how it feels," he thought, "to be a man of the Folk." He looked down at his new skin with curious eyes, noting the graceful length of his limbs; the shape of his ribs and torso; the markings on his dark skin, so like those of a Grey Seal, and yet remade into something new; and the collarbones that stood out sharply beneath the column of his neck. In the form of a Grey Seal, he was strong and powerful; but as a man he was reborn into something lithe and beautiful; and walking on the forbidden ground, with the gritty sand beneath his feet, he felt a surge of surprise and joy.

The ocean's many voices now called to him in warning. "*Beware!*" cried a herring gull, riding the wind.

"*Betrayal!*" said the voice of the wave as it crashed against a rock.

"*Come home!*" came the cry of the Grey Seal clan from the distant skerry; a cry that came from every man or woman of the selkie clan: his playmates, his brothers, his sisters.

But the selkie did not listen to them. "All I want to do is walk along the shore awhile," he told himself, folding his sealskin carefully and hiding it under a standing rock. "No-one will see me here, on the shore. The Folk are all asleep in their beds."

And he was right: nobody saw. The Folk slept, and if any dreamed of a young man naked by the shore, with long hair like a horse's mane and skin as dark as a stormy sea, they wisely did not speak of it, for such

dreams are dangerous. But when the young man of the selkie put on his sealskin to return to the people of the sea, he was conscious of a sensation almost of disappointment.

It was true that his human form was in many ways inferior to his seal Aspect. As a man he could only swim in a slow and clumsy style. It was true that, as a man, he was cold without his sealskin. It was true that as a man, his hearing and vision were both reduced, and his reflexes were slower – although they were still far keener than those of a common man of the Folk. But the thrill of walking on enemy soil – the thrill of taking the enemy's *skin* – was more than enough to compensate for any of these failings. He began to visit the Folk every night, spending longer and longer on land, and taking more risks as he became more secure in his new form, and in his new surroundings. He grew ever more daring, moving further away from the beach, and visiting the harbourside, or the settlements of the Folk, with their low-roofed houses; thick stone walls, windows facing out to sea.

He learnt that, at night, there was no-one about to question his presence or sound the alarm. His selkie senses were sharp enough to hear into the homes of the Folk. Through the walls of a fisherman's hut, he could hear the sound of a man's breathing shift from the low growl of deep sleep to the shallow murmur of wakefulness. Through the walls of a family home, he could hear the sound of an ivory comb moving through a girl's long hair, and smell the tallow candle burning at her bedside. He moved with the speed of a hunting seal; with the silence of the turning tide. And little by little, the young man of the selkie grew bolder, and more reckless.

Back at the skerry ring, the clan of the Grey Seal watched their son's movements with concern and disapproval. His mother spoke out with displeasure, saying:

"This game of yours is dangerous. No good can possibly come of it. One day you will be chief of this clan, and lead our people in my place. But for that you need to learn caution, son, and to know the ways of the enemy."

"I learn far more from watching the Folk than you ever did by hiding," replied the selkie to his mother. "This *game of mine*, as you put it, has given me the chance to see them in their natural habitat. I have looked into their homes. I have watched them with their young. I have seen that they are not the monsters that you think them to be. I think, in time, our people could even maybe become friends—"

The matriarch gave an angry bark, showing her

pointed teeth. "Young fool! Do you think you are the first of our people to have thought of this? Our history is full of young fools who thought they could befriend the Folk. And their story always ends the same way. Entrapment; enslavement; exile."

She went on to tell him many tales of selkie, robbed of their skins and sold into slavery by the Folk; unable to return to their clan; or remember their true nature; their children given human names, and thereby forever denied the chance to hear the voice of the sea, or to be with their own people.

"Even your own father," she said, "fell victim to the slavers. One of the kings of the blue salt road, lured from his people, stripped of his skin and his memories; tricked into murdering his own and damned beyond redemption. He broke my heart: and so will you, if you follow this perilous path."

But the young man was too arrogant to listen to her warnings. He knew himself to be faster, stronger, more capable than any man of the Folk. There would be time for caution when he was old, like his mother. Meanwhile, he was enjoying himself; and as time passed, and his recklessness grew, his mother's voice fell silent. His friends, too, learnt not to interfere, or risk arousing his anger. Except for one girl of the selkie, who had been his dearest friend, and who was outspoken and fearless.

"Why waste your time with the Folk?" she said. "They are poor things, paltry and pale. Their strength is only in their ships, and in their guns, and their steel harpoons. Why take their form, when in selkie skin you are strong, and lithe, and fleet, and so much more handsome than any of them?"

But the selkie said: "You are a child. When you are grown, you will understand."

The girl of the selkie said nothing, but her dark eyes flashed as she swam away. She was only a twelve-month younger than the young man of the selkie, and she was almost as fast and as strong. Angered by his arrogance, she fled to warmer waters, to play with the folk of the other clans; the Common Seals, and the Harp Seals, and the Hooded Seals, and the Bearded Seals.

The young man of the selkie watched her go with secret regret. "She will return," he told himself. "Girls are so stubborn and volatile. One day, perhaps, she will understand the ways and customs of the Folk. One day, perhaps, we will leave our skins and walk together on the shore." But he was too proud to call her back, or admit that he missed her: and so he too began to seek company elsewhere.

TWO

On an island of the Folk, there lived a young woman
called Flora McCraiceann. She was the only daughter
of a gunnerman and his wife; respectable folk of the
islands, whose only ambition was to see their daughter happily married. But, in spite of her beauty, Flora
had never fallen in love; and as she was headstrong,
demanding and proud, the young men of the island
soon found their solace elsewhere.

Her mother said: "Beware your pride. Young men
are not so plentiful that you can afford to turn them
away. If you are not spoken for by your twenty-fifth
birthday, beware; or an old maid you shall be, and
then what shall become of us?"

But Flora was undeterred. She said: "The men of
the islands are rough and uncouth. Their hands are

rough; their faces sour. I shall catch myself a prince, and bear a pretty princeling, and all the girls of the island shall envy my good fortune."

The mother said sharply: "What do you mean?" But Flora only shook her hair, which was red as a winter sunset, and said: "I shall have my princeling within the year, you wait and see." And nothing more could her mother get from her, however much she tried.

Now Flora had a grandmother living on the mainland, whose knowledge of the ocean was greater than that of any of the Folk. A widow of many years, and wise, she knew all the old tales and legends, and had passed them on to her granddaughter almost as soon as the child could talk. Tales of the Kraken, the monster that comes up from the darkest deeps to die; tales of the travelling folk of the woods, who can walk in the skins of animals. But best of all Flora had loved the old tales of the selkie, who live as seals, and can shed their skins, and take the guise of humans of singular, regal beauty.

"Once, we all lived in the sea," the grandmother had told her. "Its salt runs in our blood; our tears are memories of the ocean."

"Then why did we leave it?" Flora had said.

"Because we were fools," came the reply. "We wanted Worlds to conquer. And so we forgot the voice of the sea, and learned to walk on land, and to pretend we were more than animals."

That had been many years ago, when Flora McCraiceann was just a child. In those days the old woman had lived with her daughter and son-in-law. But the grandmother was difficult; outspoken and demanding, and her daughter had finally asked her to leave for the sake of domestic harmony. She had retired to the mainland when Flora was still very young, but Flora had always remembered her tales, and even though her childhood was past, she believed in the potency of tears.

"How can I see the selkie?" she would ask her grandmother.

And her grandmother would reply: "If a lonely maid will shed five tears into the ocean, a man of the selkie will come to her, and give her what she most desires."

And so some twenty years later, on the night of midsummer's full moon – a moon that the Folk of the islands call the Hunter's Moon – Flora went to the seashore. There she sat upon a rock, and earnestly attempted to weep. It was not an easy task. Flora was not given to weeping. But then she thought of all the young men who had failed to live up to her standards. She thought of her parents' little house, and

21

how much she longed to leave it. She thought of her twenty-fifth birthday, and how fast it was approaching. She thought of herself as an old maid, forced to stand humbly aside in church as the married women took their seats. And finally, the tears of rage and bitterness began to fall, and she hastened to the water's edge to make sure they fell into the ocean.

Five tears is all the ocean needs, according to the ancient lore. And the old lore must have been true, because no sooner had Flora dried her eyes (with a lace-trimmed handkerchief brought for the occasion) than there came a sound from behind her and, turning, she saw a strange young man standing in the water. He was tall and finely-built, with long black hair and wine-dark skin, marked with many strange tattoos of a kind she did not recognize.

For a moment her heart leaped like a fish, and she almost cried out in alarm. Then she forced herself to be still and to smile, in spite of her racing heart.

The young man was naked. It was the first time Flora had ever seen a man without his clothes on. It was entirely scandalous; and yet, in spite of her outrage, she knew that this was the selkie; the longed-for, mysterious prince of her dreams. And if this *was* a dream, she thought, then surely such things as decorum were largely unimportant.

She took off her dress and her chemise and laid them on the moonlit sand. And then she turned and stood naked before the young man of the selkie; her body white in the moonlight; clothed in nothing but her hair.

The man of the selkie looked at her; the surf around his ankles. Flora took a step forward. The sea surged white around them both. The wind was cold; the water even colder; but in spite of that, Flora felt a mysterious heat; a wildness that seemed to sing from her blood. The young man smiled and looked at her with eyes that were soft and dark as a seal's. And then, for the first time in her life, Flora McCraiceann threw decorum to the winds, and gave herself to the young man, and the moonlight, and the ocean.

Together they tumbled into the waves. Together they ran through the pounding surf. Together they lay skin-to skin on the sand and, for the very first time, it seemed that Flora McCraiceann was not entirely dissatisfied.

Three

The young man of the selkie, of course, was the son of the Grey Seal clan on one of his trips to the islands. To the girl of the Folk who had offered herself to him on the shore, he responded eagerly; enjoying the taste of her salty skin, warm against his in the cold sea; enjoying the feel of her wet hair.

Far away, on the wind, came the voice of the herring-gull: "*Beware!*"

From afar, came the sound of the wave crashing on the rocks: "*Betrayal!*"

And from the distant skerry came the call of the clan of the Grey Seal: "*Come home!*" But the young man of the selkie did not heed their warnings.

He had never been like this with any other girl of the Folk; although he had – oh, many times – with the young folk of his people. Selkie have no concept of marriage, or of faithfulness to a single partner. Selkie love freely and often, with no sense of obligation. Their children are raised by the wisest elders of the clan, while the young folk have adventures, and share in all the joys of youth.

Flora McCraiceann did not know this, of course. All she knew was that she had summoned a man, a fine, handsome man of the selkie, and that she had no intention of letting him escape. All she knew was the scent of his skin; the feel of his arms around her. She was uncertain if this was love, or simply the heat of passion; but she knew that she wanted him, and once the heat was gone from them both, her practical side reasserted itself, and she began to ask questions.

"What is your name, your clan?" she said. "I must have you meet my parents, if we are one day to be wed."

The young man of the selkie blinked in surprise. "Our people have no names," he said. "We are the selkie, that swim with the whale and the sea otter and the dolphin. My clan is the clan of the Grey Seal that lives on the ring of skerries; and your parents are no concern of mine, for our folk are sworn enemies, and they would kill me if they could."

Flora was disappointed, but in no way deterred by

the selkie's words. He might be a selkie, she told herself, but underneath he was still a man, with all a man's weaknesses and conceit. And because she wanted him (but most of all because Flora McCraiceann had always had her way in all she set out to do) she hid her displeasure and smiled at him, saying: "Meet me again tomorrow night, and see if I can't change your mind."

And so, the next night, and the following, the selkie met with Flora McCraiceann. In fact, for the next three weeks, they met every night on the little beach; and swam together in the surf, and lay together on the sand, and whispered foolish promises under the bright, uncaring stars.

Flora told the selkie of her warm house with its peat fire; of her soft bed with its linen sheets and coverlet of eiderdown. And the selkie told Flora of his life; of the bark of the seals on the rock; of the salty crunch of fish caught between his powerful jaws; of the scent of the storm, and the snap of the ice, and the many voices of the sea. And every night, Flora spoke to him of how delightful it would be for both of them to be married one day, and live in a house by the harbour, and raise beautiful, dark-eyed children.

But the selkie always laughed and said: "That is not the way of my folk," and vanished behind a nearby rock, before plunging once more into the sea. But still, Flora was undeterred. She understood the call of the sea; its freedom and its dark romance. But there was something else in her; a curious sense of *quickening*; and when she realized what it was, the urgency of her mission became even more pressing than before.

"My child will not be fatherless," said Flora McCraiceann to herself. "I shall not bear a nameless son, or have other women look at me with pity and contempt. Nor shall I do as others have done, and give my child up to the selkie; for they would claim him if they could, and take him to live in the ocean. No: my man is restless, and playful, and wild, but he must accept his duty. And if he will not give up the sea, then I will find another way to bind him to me, and his child, and curb his restlessness for good."

All this Flora said to herself as she went about her daily tasks; keeping house for her parents; going to market; going to church; working at her needlepoint – for Flora's skill with a needle was known across the islands – and waiting for the night to come, and her meeting with the selkie. And in the long sweet summer nights, while she and the selkie played in the sea, and tumbled naked on the shore, and watched the crescent moon grow fat, she dreamed of a plan to bind him to her – and to the land – forever.

Four

Summer in the northern isles lasts barely the span of a dragonfly's wing. A couple of weeks and already her face begins to turn towards winter. This year was no exception. Soon, the ice would start to creep south; the autumn gales would start to blow, and within a month the cold would be fierce and bitter.

Flora knew this all too well. Already the season was starting to turn; and her lover was less and less eager to stay with her after the lovemaking was done. Of course, without his sealskin, he was as tender as any man. Without his sealskin, the wind was cold; the sharp waves bit, and the stones were painful under-foot. If she did not act soon, she knew, the summer would be over and the sea would claim him once again. And the sea must not claim him, because he was hers, and because she wanted him. But most of all, because Flora McCraiceann had sworn to catch a prince, and bear him a pretty princeling: and that was what she meant to do; come sea, or storm, or sealskin.

Flora had never seen the sealskin, of course; the selkie always came to her in the guise of a young man. But she knew of it from stories; her grandmother had taught her well, and she knew the power of such a skin, and the knowledge that came with it. It was knowledge that had served the women of the islands well: a secret that had kept them safe, and given them healthy children. But none of the women spoke of it, not even to their loved ones, except for Flora's old grandmother, whose stories had caused her daughter to banish her to the mainland, for fear that young Flora might hear too much and be seduced by the call of the sea. It was to her grandmother's stories that Flora now returned to ensure that her man stayed loyal to her, and to their unborn child.

"To catch a selkie," her grandmother said: "find out where he keeps his sealskin. Take it, hide it away in a chest of cedarwood, bound with silver, and he will lose all memory of his clan, and the voice of the ocean, and be the slave of whomsoever has it in their keeping. But be sure to keep it safe, for if he as much as *touches* the skin, he will remember everything, and be lost to you forever."

Now Flora *had* a cedarwood chest, passed on to her by her mother on the day of her coming-of-age. It had belonged to her grandmother, over eighty years ago, and was a fine piece of craftsmanship, darkened with age, but still fragrant. So far the chest was empty, except for a few family treasures: her mother's satin wedding-dress, and her grandmother's lace one, brittle as Bible pages. Out of sentiment, perhaps, Flora's mother had always insisted that the chest be kept safely locked. But now the girl began to see another use for that cedar chest, with its silver key, just small enough to fit on a chain around her neck . . .

And so, as summer started to wane, Flora looked out for the sealskin. It was no easy task; it was her lover's most precious possession. Every night as he swam to the shore, he would hide it beneath the standing rock. Every night as he bade her farewell, he would step behind the rock, quickly unfold the sealskin and slip into the water, where he became a grey seal once more, and swam away, unnoticed.

Try as she might, Flora could never quite catch the moment at which he changed. The selkie moved too quickly, using the light on the water, or the passage of clouds over the moon as a distraction. But little by

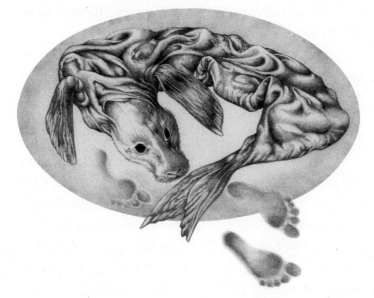

little, Flora came to realize that he never went far from the standing rock by the shore, and that, even when they were making love, his eye was always on it. And so, one moonless night, instead of meeting him in their usual spot, she hid: and when he went in search of her, she slipped behind his back, and found the sealskin under the rock, folded carefully out of sight.

The selkie was further down the beach, and did not hear her quiet approach. She took the skin from its hiding-place, and while her lover searched and called, she hid in the bushes of yellow furze that grew along the cliffside path, and listened as the selkie's cries, first coaxing, turned to anger, then became increasingly plaintive.

"Why do you flee from me, my love?" she heard him calling from the beach. "What have I done to displease you?"

Flora lay quiet in the furze, the stolen skin around her. She knew that in his selkie form, her lover would have caught her scent; heard her breathing as she lay shivering beside the path. But in his human form, he was easy to evade, and she listened to his voice as he moved to and fro on the little beach, calling to her with increasing anguish and confusion.

"What have I done?" he repeated. "Were we not happy together?" It hurt her to hear him in distress, but Flora McCraiceann told herself that this was a necessary ill. Without it, he would be gone by the first autumn gales, and she and her child would be left alone to face the scorn and contempt of her folk. Hers was a small betrayal, she thought, compared with the fate that awaited her: to give up her child to the selkie, or to live with the shame of bearing him alone. And so she hardened her heart, and when the selkie returned to his rock to find his sealskin gone, and began to search in the frantic hope that perhaps the tide had taken it, she crept silently up the cliffside path with the sealskin around her shoulders, and heard his heartbroken cry from afar as he finally realized what she had done.

"It will be over soon," she thought, as she ran towards her parents' house. "His pain will end when I lock the skin inside my mother's cedar chest – and then it will all be forgotten, and we can start our new life together."

And so, once more she hardened her heart, and put her hands over her ears to keep out the sound of her lover's voice, and locked the skin in the cedar chest under her mother's wedding-dress. And then she waited till morning – for it would not do to bring him home in the middle of the night – and when she returned to the water's edge, she found the selkie lying there naked on the stone-grey sand, blue with cold, with no memory of who he was, or how he had come to be there.

"Come with me," said Flora, handing him her fur-trimmed cloak.

And the selkie, wretched and shivering, and knowing only that she looked kind, accepted the cloak and followed her into the camp of the enemy.

Five

Barely half an hour had passed between Flora's theft of the sealskin and the loss of the selkie's memory. But in that half-hour, his rage and despair were heard by all of the clans of the north: the barrel jellyfish; the shark; the walrus and the dolphin: the albatross and the kittiwake; the grey seal and the pilot whale. But no-one knew where his sealskin had gone, and the selkie's cries rang out in vain until his memory fled from him, and he was left alone on the shore with the salt of his tears, so like that of the sea, drying on his expressionless face.

The matriarch of the Grey Seal clan heard his cry, and bowed her head, knowing that her son was lost. The herring gulls heard it, and carried it far across the sea toward the lighthouse of Sule Skerry, where the lighthouse-man heard it, and slept no more. The Harp Seals heard it, and carried it to the selkie who had been his oldest friend. And even though she was too far away to reach him before he became some-one else, she started to swim as fast as she could to the islands of the Folk – but by the time she arrived, he was gone; wrapped in Flora's fur-trimmed cloak; tame and helpless as a cub that does not see the hunter's maul.

The girl of the selkie swam up to the beach and lay there on the hard grey sand that still bore the traces of his feet and those of the woman who stole him away. She did not weep, for the shedding of tears is a habit unique to the Folk, but her heart was filled with anger and grief.

She said: "If his memory is gone, then I must remember him twice as well, and if he cannot speak for himself, then I must speak for both of us." And with that she turned and swam back out to sea, while on his island, the selkie prepared to begin his new life as a man of the Folk.

Six

The selkie walked barefoot through the streets, the fur-trimmed cloak around him. There was something about the feel of that cloak that troubled him, but it was warm, and he wrapped it tightly about him as he tried to make sense of his surroundings.

Nothing was familiar. Not the little harbour, with its docks and fishing-boats; nor the narrow, cobbled streets, lined with shops and taverns. The streets were still mostly empty (the Folk being at church) but none of the landmarks spoke to him, and the few passers-by were strangers with fish-pale skin and narrow eyes. Only the red-haired woman who had given him the cloak seemed to stir some distant memory; but it remained elusive, like a voice from far underwater.

Everything hurt. His muscles were sore; his joints

stiff; his feet were bruised and bleeding. And his head seemed full of shards of glass, reflecting scenes he could not see; and voices like a flock of birds, screaming empty warnings. But Flora took his hand in hers and led him to her parents' house; a stone-built house on top of the cliff, with a peat fire and a low roof, and windows looking out to sea.

There, she gave him a suit of clothes, a pair of boots, and a coat with a wolfskin collar, and marvelled at how handsome he was. To be sure, he still looked lost, and not as happy as she had hoped, but she told herself that this was only to be expected. He would soon settle into his new surroundings – as long as nothing reminded him of his stolen sealskin – and the sooner he did, the sooner they could begin their new life together.

And so she put the kettle on, and started to prepare her man a traditional island breakfast, while she waited for her parents – the gunnerman and his wife – to come home from church. She had her story all ready for them; and if her mother suspected that her new young man was not all he seemed, Flora felt sure that the gunnerman's wife would keep her suspicions to herself. As for her father, she told herself, he was no great thinker: as long as her man was respectful, worked hard and tried to fit in, the gunnerman would have nothing to say against his prospective son-in-law.

Meanwhile, the selkie looked around the house in growing confusion and unease. It was a neat little stone-built house, with a fire in the hearth, and a rug on the floor, and many harpoons and trophies on the walls. The selkie did not understand why these objects troubled him; and yet his mouth was dry with fear, and he shivered, in spite of the cheery fire. On every wall, there were sealskins. On every shelf, there were sharks' teeth and narwhal's horns and pieces of carved walrus ivory. The place stank of death and suffering; but the selkie, having nowhere else to go, was forced to endure it in silence.

The red-haired woman brought him food. It was greasy and strangely warm. The selkie concluded that he was unused to the food of this region. Maybe he was a stranger here. But what had become of his memory? What had become of his clothing? Had he been robbed? It seemed likely. Maybe he had been beaten – his body certainly ached enough. Maybe he had taken a blow to the head, and thereby lost his memory.

The selkie was conscious of a great surge of anger towards his unknown attackers. He found himself imagining what terrible vengeance he would take, once he recovered his memory. Was he a violent man? Perhaps. He sensed his potential for violence. What had he done, to find himself naked and alone in this place? Who were his friends, his enemies? Most of all, why did he still feel so *cold*?

The red-haired woman smiled at him, and slipped her soft white hand in his. "You are the son of a chieftain," she said, "from the islands of silk and spices. You came here on a merchant ship, carrying wares from your homeland. We met in secret, and we were betrothed without my parents' knowledge. But now the time has come to reveal our plans, and to celebrate."

"Celebrate?" said the selkie.

"I am with child," said the woman. "*Your* child. Prepare to meet your new family."

It was too much. The stench of death; the unfamiliar surroundings; the oily taste of the strange food; the aching cold that clung to him like a frozen garment; and now this revelation. The room began to spin. The selkie heard voices in his head; a thousand furious warnings in a language he no longer knew.

Flora smiled at him tenderly. "Don't worry," she said. "I'll take care of you."

The selkie shivered, in spite of the fire. Something was wrong, he told himself; something was terribly wrong with all this. Every muscle in his body cried out to him to run away. And yet there was no sign or scent of any kind of danger.

"Have some more broth," said Flora, spooning more of the greasy, warm food into the earthenware bowl by his side. Even the smell of it sickened him, but he was unable to say so in words.

He said: "What kind of broth is this?"

Flora smiled, and said; "Seal, of course. Grey seal, stewed in its own fat. You'll soon get used to the taste of it. We islanders eat it all the time."

Seven

When Flora's parents came home from church, they found their daughter taking tea with a young man in the parlour. Flora repeated her tale, with embellishments that made much of the young man's royal blood, and finally announced the exciting news of her pregnancy.

"I told you that within the year I should catch myself a prince, and bear him a pretty princeling," she said. "Now I shall be the envy of all the maids on the island, and all the young men who missed their chance will curse their evil fortune."

Her mother looked thoughtful. She knew the old tales as well as her daughter. And this young man with the seal-dark eyes seemed more than just a foreigner. She thought of the many times she had awoken in the night to hear her daughter going out; how many times Flora had missed going to church, or come down late to breakfast. She realized at once that the young man was a selkie; but at twenty-five, she told herself, a girl cannot expect to be overwhelmed with suitors.

Besides, thought the mother, a selkie would be obedient and considerate: he would never be untrue, or challenge her authority. A selkie – as long as he was tame – would be a good father, a fine hunter, and would do his best for his children. Best of all, she told herself, a selkie would always respect his mother-in-law, and work for her, and hunt for her, and care for her in her old age. And so she smiled at her daughter and said: "What a catch! I hope you know how to keep him."

To Flora's surprise, her father proved less easy to persuade. A surly man, rough-spoken, and weather-worn from years spent at sea, he looked at the selkie suspiciously from eyes as dark as the ocean.

"What is his name, his family?" the gunnerman demanded. "What gold does he bring as a bridal gift? What kind of trade does he follow?"

"He comes from far away," Flora said. "He is the son of a chieftain; his tribe, the dark-eyed, dark-skinned men of the south. And I will wed him, and bear him a son: a handsome, dark-eyed, dappled son, and take my place in church above the wives of simple seamen."

At this, the father looked angry. "What's wrong with being a seaman?" he said. "No child of mine will grow up to despise the hands that put food on her table."

The selkie, who had recognized no part of Flora's tale, said: "What exactly *is* your profession, sir?"

The father gestured proudly at the walls of the cottage, decked with trophies and souvenirs from his many travels. "I am a gunnerman," he said, "on the good ship *Kraken*, recently home from a three-month tour of the western islands. In spring, we hunt the humpback whale; the walrus and the grey seal; and

we bring back oil, and sealskins, and whalebone, and walrus ivory. And if you marry my daughter," he said, "then you, too, must find a trade, and make your living like an honest man, so that your wife and child are kept safe and well-provided for."

The selkie felt a dreadful, sick horror at the thought of hunting seal, or whale, or dolphin, or porpoise, or walrus. But with no memory of who he was, he did not know why he felt this way, or why he felt such pain and disgust at the thought of the good ship *Kraken*. So he said nothing, and tried to smile, and looked at the red-haired woman, and desperately wished that he could remember ever having loved her.

But Flora said: "Of course he must: but only when we are married; for my son must be born in wedlock, with all the respect due his family."

And so the banns were read, and the date fixed for a wedding between Flora McCraiceann and the selkie. Because he had no name of his own, she called him *Coigreach*, "the foreigner", and *McGill*, the *stranger's son*. Flora thought it a bonny name, and spent the cold autumn evenings embroidering *Flora McGill* in different kinds and colours of script over a series of linens and cloths.

The selkie tried to be grateful to the gunnerman and his wife. He tried to learn their alien ways; to eat seal

and whale-meat, as they did, even though the thought
of it horrified and disgusted him. He tried to sleep
in a bed, like the Folk; although sometimes, when he
was sleepless, he curled up on the floor and somehow
seemed to sleep better that way, though his dreams
were filled with horrors. He tried to hide his revul-
sion at the sealskins on the wall, and the other pelts
that adorned their home and the collars of their clothing. Most of all, he tried to get used to the cold that
plagued him day and night; but try as he might, it was
always there, however many clothes he wore, however close he came to the fire; as if he were missing a
layer of flesh that left him stripped and screaming.

"I used to feel the cold, like you," said the gunnerman one day. "But life on the ocean cured me of that,
as it did of so many things. Now I feel it no more than
I feel the sting of the spray against my cheek; or the
sickness that all sailors endure the first week on board
their vessel." And he brought out a dusty bottle of
rum, and poured them both a generous dram, and
laughed when the selkie spluttered and choked, and
said: "Here's to you, Coigreach McGill. I swear we'll
make a man of you yet!"

But as the year waned, and his memory still showed
no sign of returning, the selkie began to realize that his
old life was gone for good; that he would never be at

ease in his skin, nor would he ever cease to feel that dizzy rush of fear whenever the gunnerman spoke of the whaler. However much he tried, he could not get used to drinking rum, or wearing the skins of animals, or eating the flesh of the grey seal, or sleeping in a feather bed. But at least he learnt to pretend a tolerance he did not feel; and to smile when it was expected of him, and to laugh at the gunnerman's jokes, and the gunnerman and his wife declared that he was a fine, upstanding young man, a credit to the family.

And so time passed, and the wedding drew close, and Flora embroidered her bridal trousseau, and day by day, the selkie began to feel a sense of creeping dread. Something was coming, he understood; something that would test him hard; and as the day of the wedding approached, he could not eat, nor could he sleep without the most terrible nightmares.

"'Tis nothing but nerves," said the gunnerman, when Flora's mother expressed her concern at the dark circles under the eyes of her prospective son-in-law. "Do you remember the day we were wed? I could scarce put two words together." And the gunnerman laughed, and clapped the selkie on the back, and said: "Be brave, Coigreach McGill. A wedding only lasts a day. Soon this nonsense will be done, and you and I will be free to go."

"Free?" said the selkie.

"Aye," he said. "For I have spoken to the Captain of the good ship *Kraken*. He has agreed to take you on as an apprentice gunner – under my supervision, of course – to sail as soon as the weather permits. It is a proud and noble trade, and one that will earn you the respect of every man on the island, as it must, for Flora is my only child, and must have the best of everything."

The selkie smiled, but his lips were numb and his belly filled with ice. "A gunner?" he said. "What exactly does a gunner do?"

"He works the harpoon," said the gunner, his eyes as dark as the ocean. "And I swear there is no finer work; no, not in the whole of the Nine Worlds. Just stay with me, and watch what I do, and you'll be like me in no time at all." And once more he laughed, and poured rum for them both, and drank to the health of his new son-in-law, and the selkie smiled and drained the glass, but inside he was shivering.

Part 2

≈

Then ane arose at her bed fit
And a grumly guest I'm sure was he,
Saying; "Here am I, thy bairn's father,
Although I am not comely."

Child Ballad, no. 133

One

The matriarch of the Grey Seal clan had learnt of her son's misadventure with grief and resignation. Now she accepted his unhappy fate. As far as she was concerned, he was lost; forever cut off from his people, his knowledge of their language gone; never to return to the sea.

Some of his friends tried to argue that there was still hope; that he could be saved if only his sealskin could be found. But the matriarch was proud, and would not listen to their pleas, and she bared her teeth and hardened her heart and forbade them to go near the islands.

"He is one of the Folk now," she said. "To approach him would be dangerous. He would not recognize you now: he might even hunt you down."

And so the selkie kept away; except for the girl of the Grey Seal clan, who could not bear to see him alone, abandoned by his people. Every day she would swim to the beach where she had seen his tracks, and although it was too cold for her to shed her sealskin and take human form, she watched from afar for a glimpse of him.

But all the Folk looked the same to her, in their bulky winter coats and fur-lined hats and sealskin boots. All the Folk looked the same to her, just as all seals looked the same to them, and even if she had seen him, she knew he would not have recognized her.

On the island, the winter had come; a great dark cloud that froze the land, and froze the sea, and froze the hearts of the islanders. The sun went down and did not come up; nor would it until springtime. Instead, there was almost perpetual night, except for a couple of hours before dawn – a dawn that never really broke, but promised, and promised, turning the sky crimson and gold, then slipping away into darkness. The selkie knew of this, of course; but in winter the grey seals followed the sun and the warmer currents to the south; and stayed there, feeding well on the shoals of herring and mackerel and cuttlefish until the sun returned. The Folk did not go south, of course, but simply endured the darkness, as snow fell over the mountaintops, and ice crept like a spider's web all around the islands.

A midwinter wedding, said Flora McCraiceann, was just the thing to cheer them up. Her wedding trousseau was finished at last: a dozen sheets and pillowcases, with her initials embroidered over them in cherry silk. With that, six nightgowns, four chemises, sundry underthings and two dozen lawn handkerchiefs made up the trousseau, locked away in the cedar chest that she kept in her bedroom. It was the very same cedar chest in which she had hidden the sealskin, almost four months ago to the day, and Flora kept the silver key on a chain which she wore around her neck, for she had no intention of letting her man anywhere near that skin, ever again.

To be sure, the selkie was no longer the man with whom she had tumbled in the surf. The wildness had gone from him, and the joy. Instead he was humble, uncertain; respectful of Flora's parents; trying hard to fit in with their ways. He went to church; he helped in the home; he tried to be like other men. But his love for her, and his passion, were gone as surely as his memory, leaving only gratitude, duty and affection.

A part of her grieved for the man she had loved. And yet it suited her to see him obedient, docile and eager to please. Passion is unpredictable. It does not behave or obey as it should. But while the sealskin was in her possession, she knew he would remain hardworking and respectful; and that she would bear his child, and be the envy of the other girls.

Girls were not much valued in the island communities. As maidens, they were courted and wooed, but as fishermen's wives, they served their men, and cooked for them, and cleaned their homes, and worked, and raised their children. Flora had no intention of ever being such a fisherman's wife: and the thought that the selkie would be her slave forever was attractive. To be sure, she sometimes felt a little uneasy at what she had done. But then she told herself that he had forced her to make the decision: that he would have left her and her child alone if she had not acted first. Besides, could he really be suffering if he did not remember what he had lost?

"I did him a favour," she told herself. "In a way, I rescued him. Among the selkie he was nothing but a savage; an animal, with no knowledge of God, no education, no decency. It's only like breaking a horse," she thought, "or training a wolf cub to run with the dogs." And the more she told herself these things, the less her conscience troubled her, and the more she came to believe her actions had really been quite selfless.

Day by day the wedding approached; and the child

in her belly grew and grew, and Flora McCraiceann felt increasingly pleased with herself, and with her plans for the future. Her mother knitted baby clothes and prepared for the day of the wedding; and her father, still blithely unaware that his prospective son-in-law was a selkie, counted the days and weeks until he could go to sea again; for the sea was his secret love; and the hunt his only real joy.

TWO

At last, the day of the wedding arrived. Midwinter's Eve; a day declared propitious by the village priest. Everyone on the island was there to watch Flora McCraiceann wed the selkie, and the celebrations would have lasted from sunrise to sunset, if the sun had risen at all.

Instead, it lasted from low tide to high, then back again to low tide, and began with a dinner of many delicate courses: sour herring; cuttlefish pie; roast seal in a sea-salt crust; fricassee of whalemeat; rock oysters; sea-urchins in their shells, and to finish with, a glorious cake, shaped like a whaling-ship in full sail, with the rigging picked out in white icing and the mast in green angelica. To make up for the absence of sunlight, there were a thousand candles lighting the church from altar to nave; and the bride wore a dress and matching cap made from the skins of baby seals; as soft and white as new-fallen snow.

The selkie spent his wedding day in a daze of anguish and confusion. The people; the candles; the clothing; the dancing; the food – everything seemed designed to cause him pain and discomfort. His own bridal outfit, made from the pelts of white wolves from the mainland, was already enough to sicken him; but that of his bride was far, far worse. Worse still was the fact that he did not know *why* he was thus affected: the others seemed to find the wearing of animal skins a perfectly natural thing to do. He ate almost nothing at the table, except for a couple of urchins and some oysters which, being raw, did not disgust him as did the cooked food; and though he did not touch the wine, he sat through the meal with aching limbs and a pounding headache.

The gunnerman saw his discomfort and said: "Don't worry. It'll be over soon. These fancy parties aren't to my taste either. Men like you and I would sooner be at sea than on dry land, hunting the seal and the walrus." He laughed at the selkie's expression, saying: "I was very like you once. When I was young and foolish. But going to sea made a man of me. And it will make a man of you, too. I'll see to that!" And he poured himself more ale, and drank, while the selkie tried not to shudder.

The gunnerman's wife was in high spirits, too. Kicking up her skirts, she laughed and danced as wild as a witch in May, and drank more ale than anyone, including the gunnerman himself. Silver gleamed at her throat as she danced, and her face grew increasingly flushed, and she sang:

> *"Three cheers for the bride and the bridegroom!*
> *Three cheers for the folk of the sea!*
> *And three cheers for the cedar chest,*
> *That was the maid's only dowry!"*

But no-one *really* heard what she sang – except for the grandmother of the clan, who had come over from the mainland. No-one had invited her, and no-one marked her presence among so many merrymakers.

But it was she who had taught the bride all about the selkie; and now, as she heard her daughter's song, her eyes widened in understanding.

She looked at the groom; unsmiling in his wolf-skins, his hair bound back. She looked at the bride in her sealskin robe, her hair like a coronet of red gold under the little sealskin cap. And now, under the wedding-dress, which was made from the white

THE BLUE SALT ROAD

skins of baby seals, she saw the gleam of a silver chain – and on the silver chain, a key – that the old woman recognized.

Standing with some difficulty, for she was as old as the skerries themselves the grandmother went over to greet the happy couple. For a moment, the selkie looked into the eyes of the grandmother of the clan. They were dark, and very bright, and filled with ancient mischief, and it occurred to him that they reminded him of someone – though who it was, he did not know – and his heart swelled with longing for something, or maybe it was *somewhere*, that he had forgotten.

The grandmother said: "What a handsome pair. The King and Queen of Fiddler's Green would not have made a finer."

"I made the bridal clothes myself," said Flora, with a brilliant smile (although inside, she was a little fearful of the old lady, and of what she might say to the bridegroom).

"Aye," said the grandmother. "You always were quick with a needle. Be quick now with the wine-jug, and fetch an old lady a glass of wine to pay for her long journey."

The bride reluctantly went off in search of wine, and the old woman was left with the selkie. For a moment

their eyes met; his as dark as a stormy sea; hers as dark as the hearts of the Folk.

"Tell, me, do I know you?" said the selkie at last to the crone.

"I doubt it," said the old lady, "although in part, I may be the cause of your current circumstance. If so, I am sorry for it; for to be lucky in love is not always to be equally lucky in marriage. Had I but known that, years ago, I might not have been so quick to pass on the fruits of my experience. Now those fruits are ripening, and I fear their taste will be sour."

"I don't understand," said the selkie.

"Of course not," said the grandmother. "But I once knew a man of your kind. A traveller on the blue salt road. Handsome he was, like you, and lost; and like you, soon to be wedded. In tears he was summoned, salt as the sea. In silver was his binding. In blood and betrayal, his calling he found. In cedar his salvation."

The selkie looked at her eagerly, having understood nothing but the fact that the old woman knew a man of his kind. "Did he tell you from what land he came? Did he tell you the name of his clan?"

The old woman shook her head. "It was a long time ago," she said. "And I am old and forgetful. But remember the old adage, young man. They don't call it 'wedlock' for nothing."

63

The bride came back at that moment, bearing an earthenware pitcher of wine, and looked sharply at the grandmother. "My grandmother likes to tell stories," she said. "She has more tales in her head than wit. Do not heed her foolish words, but dance with me, for are we not the happiest folk of all the islands?" And she swept the selkie away into the throng of revellers, and left the old lady to her thoughts, which were as deep as the open sea, and as cold as midwinter.

Three

Weeks passed, and winter clenched its white fist on the islands. Folk stayed in their houses as snow fell as high as the windows. There was no fishing to be had, except through the ice in the harbour; and the fishing-boats were in dry dock lest the ice crush their hulls to pieces.

The long winter night had already brought thirty days of darkness. The stars shone at noon, and the northlights drew their green curtain over the sea. The seals had moved south to their feeding-grounds; the birds had flown to follow the sun. But the selkie remained; perpetually cold in spite of his layers of clothing; fingers numb; teeth clenched; sleepless and hungry and miserable. He hated the gunnerman's house, although his hearth was warm and welcoming; and in spite of the cold, would often roam in the blue false dawn, outside in the fallen snow, or on the beach, where the wind screamed at the sea like an angry woman.

The selkie could stay there for hours, shivering, but strangely at ease, though he often found himself close to tears at the sight of an osprey in flight, or a barrel jellyfish cast up on the frozen beach. Once or twice by the seashore, he thought he saw the round head of a grey seal bobbing up between the waves; but the Grey Seals were gone to warmer climes, and besides, the animal was always gone before he could be sure of what he had seen.

As for Flora, she stayed indoors, making clothes for her unborn child, using the white skins of baby seals killed by her father on his last trip around the skerries. The passion that had driven her into the selkie's arms had waned, to be replaced by a different sensation. Her thoughts were all for the child now growing in her belly: and even on her wedding-night, when the selkie had shyly attempted to interest her in lovemaking, she had turned away from him, saying: "Not with a baby on the way." A half-truth perhaps, but kinder than telling him that he had changed, and that his tentative approach did nothing to kindle her desire. The *real* truth was that Coigreach McGill, though passable husband material, had none of the wildness and energy of a nameless selkie. They lay together side-by-side, no longer as lovers, but as friends, and when the selkie moaned in his sleep, Flora would comfort him like a child, and whisper reassurances, and tell herself that it was because this new life was still strange to him, and that he would soon adjust to it.

Besides, for the first time in her life, Flora was truly happy. The child in her belly was nearly half-grown, and she had no doubt that it would be a son. Already she could feel his presence; his hunger; his eagerness. Already she knew that he would be dark, with his father's seal-brown eyes. And already she felt a love for him that she had never known before; a love that eclipsed everything else. She, who had been hard and proud, now felt a new softness inside her; and she wondered at the change in herself.

"I wonder," she thought, "what my son will become? A sailor? A soldier? A gunnerman?" But none of these seemed appropriate for the child of Flora McGill. Her child was born for greater things. Her child would see the world, travel far, live long, have marvellous adventures. Why else would she feel this way? Why else would she have gone to the sea to catch herself a selkie?

Four

John McCraiceann, the gunnerman, had tried to warm to his son-in-law. But the selkie had found it hard to suppress his dislike of Flora's father. Perhaps it was the smell of rum and death that seemed to cling to the gunnerman; or the eager way he spoke of his love of hunting.

"As soon as this ice melts, we'll sail again," he would say to the selkie. "You'll soon learn, there's nothing finer or nobler than life aboard a whaler. The sting of the spray, the roar of the sea, the humpback whale in his death throes, churning the sea into a cauldron of blood, and the warm red rain a-falling."

"Noble? Fine?" said the selkie, trying vainly to hide his disgust.

The gunnerman laughed. "You're squeamish," he

said. "I understand. But there's a beauty to the whaling life, once you get accustomed to it. There's beauty, and danger, and freedom – freedom like you've never known. And the enemy is a worthy foe, leading us on a desperate dance between the cheerless skerries. There are grey seals as big as a man, with teeth like those of a timber wolf; and they are wild and mettlesome, and fierce in defence of their young."

"I daresay you would be, in their place," said the selkie.

The gunnerman laughed. "They're animals. Wild animals. On Sule Skerry a twelvemonth ago, I saw a man fall to a bitch seal who tore him apart the way a child might tear a rag doll asunder. And there are worse things than seals out there—" The gunnerman's voice grew fierce and low. "For those skerries are home to the selkie; creatures that look like seals by day, but by night take the form of human beings and walk among our folk unseen. Some say they're a legend, but *I* know they're among us: seducing our women; corrupting our men; cursed, Godless and vicious."

The selkie listened intently to this description of his people. Of course, he had no memory of his life with the Grey Seal clan; and yet he knew in his heart that the tale was true. The selkie were real. They existed.

He felt a sudden sadness mixed with a strange excitement, imagining the seal folk; free and fierce and wild as the waves.

He said: "Then how can you know if a seal you killed was an ordinary seal, or one of these selkie you speak of?"

The gunnerman said: "You can't know for sure. But sometimes there's something in the eyes. And if you see it, strike first, and strike fast. Those animals would strip your hide just as fast as you'd take theirs; and how could I ever face Flora again, knowing I didn't save you?"

The gunnerman laughed, but the selkie did not. And that night, as he lay in bed, he dreamed of swimming in the sea, and in his dream he did not feel the cold, but was strong, and powerful, and free. And at his side another swam; a Grey Seal, sleek and beautiful. And the Grey Seal sang to him in a voice that seemed to fill the emptiness inside him as nothing else had before: and in his dream he understood the words the Grey Seal sang:

> *We who once were kings and queens*
> *A-begging now we go*
> *Among the fields of ocean green*
> *And in the burning snow.*

THE BLUE SALT ROAD

In borrowed skin and borrowed clothes
We frolic and make merry
Beggars on the blue salt road
The salt road to Sule Skerry.

Five

Time passed; and the winter waned, and the sun returned to the islands. Slowly the snow began to melt, and the grip of the ice over the sea began to break, until finally the gunnerman announced that the *Kraken* was due to set sail for a three-month tour of the skerries.

"For when the seals come north again," he said, "they are fat and ready to breed; and their pelts are glossy and winter-thick, and will fetch a high price at the market." He looked hard at the selkie and said: "And if you are to have a home of your own, and support your wife and family, you will need to work as I do, and bring home skins, and oil, whalebone and walrus ivory."

The selkie knew the gunner was right. But though

his father-in-law was impatient to see him join the *Kraken*'s crew, Flora was not as eager. One night, when she thought he was asleep, the selkie overheard her arguing with her parents.

"Why must he go to sea so soon?" she said. "Why not wait till the child is born?"

"The boy must learn to be a man," said the voice of the gunnerman. "Besides, he needs to earn his keep. How else can he care for his family?"

Flora's voice was plaintive. "Surely there are other jobs more suited to his character?"

Now came the sharp voice of the mother-in-law. "Your father went to sea," she said, "as did his father before him. Why should your man be different?"

"Because he's mine," said Flora.

The mother-in-law laughed at that. "Let him choose his way," she said. "You can't keep him here forever."

This was true, the selkie thought. However much he might dislike the thought of being on a whaling-ship, the call of the open sea was strong, and he could not face another winter living with his parents-in-law. Flora's belly was growing round. The child would be born by May-day. Time enough for him to return with gold enough to pay his way. *Time enough for you to escape*, said a dry voice in his mind, and although the selkie did not know to whom the voice belonged, it held enough authority for him to believe it spoke the truth. But – *escape*? He was not a prisoner. He was with the woman he loved, who was carrying his child. Agreed, he had lost his memory, but what kind of life had he had before that? And what kind of man leaves his wife and child for the sake of a few dreams?

"What are these dreams?" said Flora, one night as the selkie lay sleepless, afraid to close his eyes and shivering in the darkness.

"I dream of the sea," said the selkie. "But in my dream, I am not myself, nor am I alone." Flora seemed to stiffen at this. "Who else is with you, then?" she said.

"I do not know," said the selkie. "But she and I swim together, with no fear of the hunter's lance. And in my dream I understand the language of the ocean, and it calls to me in a voice so sad that it almost breaks my heart."

"Your heart?" said Flora. "Your heart belongs to me, and to our unborn child."

"I know," said the selkie. "But in my dreams –"

"Enough of your dreams," said Flora. And turning away, she pretended to sleep, and the rest of the night passed in silence.

≈

And so on the day of the Wolf Moon, the selkie pre-pared to board the *Kraken*, along with John McCraice-ann and the rest of the whaler's crew. A sixty-foot sloop, with two whaleboats and a crew of twenty-one, including the gunnerman himself. The Captain and his first mate had cabins over the main deck, and the selkie bunked with the rest of the men, deep in the belly of the ship.

To his surprise the selkie found the gunnerman was unexpectedly popular among the crew. All the men respected him, and wanted to meet his new son-in-law. The selkie suddenly found himself surrounded by curious faces. Everyone wanted to shake his hand; to buy him a drink; to be his friend. The gunner-man had already spoken of the comradeship of his fellow-crew members, but the selkie had not expected such a demonstration of warmth, and for the first time, he began to believe that maybe this trip would prove less of an ordeal than he had feared.

They set off from the harbour at dawn, one chilly morning in February. The selkie remained with the gunnerman, who had promised the Captain to train him, and they set sail northwards into the mists to the hunting-grounds of the islanders. The selkie came to realize that his was a privileged status: as an apprentice gunner (but most of all as John McCraiceann's son-in-law), he was entitled to greater respect; improved rations; an extra blanket on his bunk. With these privileges came a sense of expectation: an under-standing that he would be an asset to the crew. The selkie was uncertain – he still felt sick at the thought of killing a whale – but the gunnerman seemed confident that he would acquit himself like a man. And so the *Kraken* sailed north; and although the selkie missed the security of his life with Flora, he found he was happier than at any time over the past five months, although he was unable to say what it was that had changed in him.

The northernmost islands cover a span of around three hundred miles. There are seventeen larger islands in the archipelago, clustered into three main groups, the nearest of which lies thirty miles or there-abouts from the mainland. Beyond that, and spread out to the north, there are the skerries; bleak outcrops of rock, inhabited only by sea-birds and seals, and of course, the selkie.

All these skerries have names, although the selkie seldom use them. The folk of the sea have no use for names, or for the ownership they imply. Selkie have no possessions, no understanding of property. But the Folk give names to everything: every road; every village and town; every rocky outcrop. Rivers have names; and lakes; and seas; and everything that lives therein. Thus the Folk manage to fool themselves into thinking that they are the masters of everything.

Of course, the selkie knew nothing but the name of their destination. Sule Skerry was only a mouthful of sounds to him, without any deeper meaning. But as the *Kraken* left the coast of the island and made for the open sea, the selkie was conscious of a growing sense of both familiarity and of nostalgia.

"I have been here before," he thought, as he watched from his place on the deck. "This is a road I have travelled, in the days when I had my memory."

It was a surprisingly powerful thought. His memory was there, he knew; submerged like the wreck of some great ship; half-buried in the ocean floor; its broken masts draped with great dark ragged swags of weed: rainbow wrack and sugar kelp and dead man's bootlaces. If only he could see it through the fathoms of green water! But try as he might, the selkie could not; and the *Kraken* sailed on regardless.

Life aboard the ship was hard, and the work was heavy and exhausting. The selkie's hands bled from the hempen ropes, but in spite of that and the cramped conditions, he slept better at sea than he ever had on land, and dreamed of swaying forests of weed, and shimmering curtains of herring. Other men suffered from seasickness, but the selkie felt far more secure on the rolling deck of the ship than he ever had on shore. And though the rest of the crew complained about the rations aboard the ship, the selkie preferred the dry salt fish and hard biscuit to the greasy stews of whale-meat and seal prepared so lovingly by his wife.

"You're a natural," said the gunnerman. "Steady on deck as you are on land. Stay close to me, and watch what I do, and you'll soon be as skilled as I am."

By then, they had been six days at sea, with little chance of hunting. But on the seventh day the lookout spotted a pod of pilot whales to starboard; the order was given; the whaleboats lowered, and at last, the hunt began.

Part 3

≈

I am a man upon the land
I am a silkie in the sea,
And when I'm far frae every strand,
My home it is in Sule Skerry.

Child Ballad, no. 113

One

In spite of the matriarch's warnings, the wilful girl of the Grey Seal clan had gone in pursuit of the *Kraken*. It was she who had sung to the selkie in his dreams; she whom he had glimpsed from the beach. From her refuge under the waves, she had watched him, and grieved for him still, and hoped that something would happen to help restore his memory. But nothing – not even an ocean voyage – would serve to recover his sense of self as long as the stolen sealskin was kept safe in the cedar chest.

Now she watched as two whaleboats were lowered from the *Kraken*'s side: each suspended by its belly-strap and hanging from its davits, each with its crew of six oarsmen. Each boat was thirty feet in length, and painted primrose-yellow. Each one carried lances, and fluke-spades, and two great tubs of hempen rope, with a piggin of water set by in case the line began to smoke as it unspooled in the wake of the stricken whale.

The selkie was in the second boat, but although she tried to catch his eye, he was too preoccupied with the hunt to pay her any attention. And so she observed the scene from afar, taking care to stay well away from the boats. Whale was their quarry today, she knew; but another day it might easily be seal, or shark, or dolphin. The Folk were vicious, she knew: and while the selkie was under their spell, he was capable of anything.

The pilot whale is not a true whale, but one of the dolphin family. They are playful creatures and often gather around ships, which makes them easy prey for the Folk, who value them for their meat and oil. These pilot whales were on their way to their feeding-grounds north of the islands; a group of some four or five families, with youngsters in tow and the great matriarch of the clan bringing up the rear.

The whaleboats were light and manoeuvrable, each with its mast and single sail, and the long oars speeding its progress. The gunner rode, lance poised, on the bow of his boat, while the oarsmen moved into position, manning the oars, and ready to manoeuvre the craft into just the right position for the gunner to strike. The second boat moved to head off the pod and to drive the creatures towards them.

The sun was in the selkie's eyes as the boat moved forward. Bright spray shot up from the bows, filling the air with diamonds. The salt of his sweat and the salt of the sea were indistinguishable, and the song of the pilot whales reached him over the sound of the wind, so like something he might once have dreamed and, waking, half-forgotten. Of course the selkie no longer knew the language of the pilot whales, but to him they sounded both merry and sad; their voices like the voice of the sea. He longed to call to them – *Dive! Dive!* – but he said nothing, and watched, and was frozen.

Pilot whales are curious, and instead of moving away from the boats, circled around to investigate. The selkie was silent in horror, but the gunner seemed unmoved. Instead he turned to the selkie, and held out the lance to him and said: "Hold it, boy, and strike at my word."

The selkie said nothing, and did not move. For a second the point of the gunnerman's lance shone between them like ice in the sun.

"What's wrong, man?"

The selkie shook his head. "I cannot."

The gunner watched him a moment more, then turned away, saying: "Watch what I do. Next time you will be better prepared."

The pilot whales were closer now; their curious eyes on the men in the boat. One in particular was close; a young adult male that swam playfully under and around the boat.

Waiting his moment, the gunnerman aimed; he struck; and then the sea was white and red and thrashing with activity. The yellow whaleboat heaved and lurched and rocked as the stricken whale tried to escape; but the lance had gone into its spine, and the creature was dying. It gave a long, deep sigh from its blowhole, spouting blood rain into the air. The blood was warm, and fine as mist, and it covered the men in the whaleboat in a sheet of scarlet. For a moment the mournful brown eyes of the whale met the eyes of the selkie, and for an instant the selkie thought he saw a look of *recognition*—

And then there was no time to do anything but follow orders; to bring up the oars; to attach the float to the dead whale, and to pursue the rest of the pod as at last – too late, too late – they understood the danger.

The men took four whales that morning. A good catch, said the Captain: and between the flensing of

the skin, and the rendering of the oil in the whaler's copper try-pots, and the salting of the flesh for storing and sale in harbour, the men were all kept busy for the rest of the day. The selkie did what he was told in a kind of bubble: soundless, nerveless and numb. That evening, as the rest of the crew celebrated the day's catch with singing and rum and merriment, he fled sickly to his straw bed, and tried to sleep, and could not; then tried not to awaken, and could not.

The gunnerman was patient, although his dark eyes showed anger. Once more he told the selkie: "I was like you, when I was still green. I thought the whales were calling me. I thought I heard their voices at night. But I soon learned, and you will too, that we are masters of the sea. Its creatures feed and serve us. It has always been this way. The king of the blue salt road does not concern himself with the beggars."

The selkie looked at him with surprise. Something about that phrase had awakened a fleeting memory in him. Maybe something the old woman had said, on the night of his wedding – the old woman who had seemed to know something about his people. That night he had been too confused to pay attention to her words: and in the morning she had gone, taking her secrets with her.

His mind went back to what she had said. The selkie remembered it clearly now. It sounded almost like poetry:

> *In tears he was summoned, salt as the sea,*
> *In silver was his binding.*
> *In blood and betrayal, his calling he found.*
> *In cedar, his salvation.*

"Is this ship made of cedarwood?" the selkie asked the gunnerman.

The gunner looked puzzled. "Not that I know of. Our ships are made of mainland oak; weatherproof and sturdy. Why?"

The selkie shrugged. "No reason," he said. "Maybe it was something I dreamed."

TWO

They sold their kill the following day at the port of a neighbouring island. The *Kraken* was not a large enough ship to carry all their takings, and so they sold the meat while it was fresh, and moved north towards the outer skerries, where the ice was still melting. The bigger whales – the humpback, the bowhead – could sometimes be caught against the ice: and the walrus and seal would be easy prey, stranded; surrounded by hunters.

The selkie did not follow the rest of the crew on shore. He stayed on board the *Kraken*, silently watching from the bows as the Folk came and went. He felt no connection to these men, who talked and drank and laughed and swore; when only twenty-four hours ago they had murdered four gentle, intelligent creatures.

Only John McCraiceann, the gunnerman, seemed aware of his trouble, but offered no comfort, simply repeating what he had said: that the selkie would soon get accustomed to it.

"You need to make a kill, boy. It's the only way you'll get over it. You've seen me at work. Your balance is good. There's no reason you shouldn't soon be as skilled as I am with a lance. And once you've tasted the joy of the kill—" at this the selkie closed his eyes "–then you'll be a hunter – a man – and you'll have no more of these womanish doubts."

But as the journey north went on, the selkie's doubts only increased. Three weeks out, and the *Kraken* had taken two more pilots and four basking sharks – three adults and a juvenile – and both times, the selkie had found himself unable to make the kill. Both times, the gunner had covered for him, leaving him the job of dealing with the carcasses, which the men stripped and boiled down for oil in the same copper try-pots they had used before. It was a sickening task: and yet the selkie preferred it to the company of the men. Alone, he did not need to disguise his loathing of their cargo. Alone, he could hide away and mourn, without attracting the attention of the other crewmen.

Whale oil is better than shark oil, he learned. But the oil of one of the larger whales was better than

that of an orca or pilot whale. The finest grade of oil could only be taken from the humpback, the bow-head, the sperm, the baleen, which could only be found in the colder waters, close to the frill of ice that clung to the northernmost skerries. The selkie could only shiver at the thought of killing one of these crea-tures – creatures that lived for hundreds of years; that sang to him from the open sea – and even though he avoided them, the other crewmen sensed his disgust, and looked at him with unspoken contempt.

"Next time, you must use the lance," the gunner told him urgently. "I will show you where to strike. And afterwards, you'll be one of us, and the other men will respect you again. You started out so well," he went on. "You seemed to be taking well to the life of a seaman. But these airs and graces you give yourself – as if you thought you were better than they. Whalers are a clan, boy. This is no way to be part of it."

The selkie had never felt more alone, or less inclined to belong to a clan. But the gunner insisted, saying to him: "The men don't like, or trust you, boy. They think you are arrogant and aloof. You never laugh or drink with them, or share in their conversations. Worse yet, you've not made a kill. They're starting to say you're a clocker."

"A clocker?" said the selkie.

"Aye," said the gunner. "A hoodie-claw. A clocker, a slippie, a pickmaw. Bad luck is what it means, and when a man starts to be bad luck, the rest of the crew knows what to do. You'd better do as I say, boy, and try to fit in with the rest of the men; or you'll soon find yourself in trouble."

"What trouble?" said the selkie.

The gunner looked at him closely. "I once knew a man," he said at last. "A bad-luck man, a clocker who thought he was better than those around him. Too grand to drink with the other men: too fine to dirty his hands like the rest. One night, they dragged him from his bunk, and stripped him, and tied him hand

and foot: and then they hauled him in chains around the keel, so that he was all ripped and blooded. The Captain turned a blind eye. He knew not to intervene. Men of the islands know what to do with a man who doesn't want to fit in. Mark my words: you want to fit in. I say this to you for my daughter's sake, and for the sake of her unborn son."

The selkie considered the gunner's words. Although he sensed no affection there, the man had always been kind to him. And he was right: his new bride was waiting for him at home, and he needed to learn a trade to help support his family. His memory might never return. And even if it did, he had a greater responsibility.

And so, that night, instead of going to sleep as soon as his duties allowed him, he stayed awake with the other men, and drank himself into a stupor, and laughed at jokes he did not understand, and applauded tales of slaughter, and finally awoke at dawn with a parched throat and a headache to the sound of the lookout calling:

"Blows! Blooooows!"

Three

It was a pod of bowhead whales; two adults and a juvenile. The bowhead is a gentle creature, but can be fierce in defence of its young. The *Kraken* had entered cold waters by then: though not cold enough to ensure that the whales could be trapped against the creeping ice. The cry went out: and the selkie, still dazed from the after-effects of too much island whisky, found himself being slapped awake and dragged along by the gunnerman towards the *Kraken*'s whaling-boats, which were ready to drop into the sea as soon as the Captain gave the word.

The gunnerman looked at the selkie. "Now's your chance, boy," he told him. "Ride behind me till I give the word, and I'll show you where to strike."

The gunnerman took his place in the bows, with the selkie sitting behind him. The whaleboat hit the waves with a great salt smack of water, showering the crewmen. The spray turned to salty sleet as it fell; it stung the selkie's face like hail, and his heart was afraid as they started to row towards the pod of bowhead whales. The creatures, sensing danger, veered away into the path of the second whaleboat, and for a moment the selkie was sure that they, not he, would make the kill. But the juvenile was slow. Passing between the whaling-boats, it hesitated, breaching and breasting the wave and lashing its large flat tail in distress. Then it turned from the second boat and made straight for the one in which the selkie and the gunnerman were waiting.

Even a juvenile bowhead whale can put a whaleboat in danger. The creature heading for their boat was over ten times as heavy. The selkie saw its eye roll as it slipped into the wave: then it was under the surface, and he could see its smooth dark hide, all filigreed with barnacles, like a great rock in the shallows, but moving at tremendous speed.

The gunner cried out: "Put up the oars!"

The men at the oars stopped rowing and lifted the oars from the water. Below, the great grey hide of the whale, moving fast underneath them. It grazed the keel, and the selkie heard a sound from the men, a long, soft sigh of fear and anticipation.

The gunnerman turned to the selkie. "It means to come up under the keel: to use its tail to capsize us. When I give you the word, boy, strike exactly where I tell you."

The selkie shook his head as the man held out the lance for him to take.

The gunnerman lowered his voice. "You must. The men are watching. You must make a kill today, or suffer the consequences."

The selkie took the lance. It was attached to a spring mechanism, coiled tightly against the bow. The end of the lance was attached to a rope. The point was steel, and deadly.

"Await my call," said the gunnerman. His voice was low and tender. The selkie thought he had never seen the man look so happy, or so intent. The joy of the hunt was on him now: his eyes were pinned with strange fire.

In silence they waited, all of them. The men at the oars said never a word. Their breathing was hushed; their faces pale.

Underneath the little boat, the whale seemed to go on forever. Deeper and deeper it went, until it was barely visible any more, except as a shadow under the

boat, deep and dark and threatening. Then it began to resurface fast. The gunner was right, the selkie thought. It meant to come up under them. If it did, it would lift the boat and smash it with its powerful tail. The crewmen – if they did not drown – would be at its mercy. And yet the selkie was not afraid. Instead, he felt a kind of hope; a kind of exhilaration.

Save yourself, he told the whale. *Swim, and keep on swimming.* Every muscle tensed and taut, he watched, the lance forgotten. From under the water, he could hear the voices of the bowhead whales calling to their lost child; it sounded like singing.

The gunner turned to the selkie as the whale neared the surface. "There's a place behind its ear," he told the selkie quietly. "You'll see it just for a moment, boy: and when you do, that's where you'll strike. Strike fast and strike hard, and then it will be over: and afterwards we'll all be rich, and you will be a gunnerman."

The selkie felt his heart beat even faster than before. His eyes were filled with sea spray; his arms ached from holding the lance. And then the whale surfaced; the gunnerman cried: "*Now! Shoot!*" and the selkie made his shot: but he did not aim for the spot by the ear that the gunner had described. Instead he closed his eyes and let the lance fly just a shade too soon: it missed the bowhead's neck and flew free, shooting out the coil of rope with a rattling like Lord Death's carriage on its way to Netherworld.

There came a cry from the throats of the men like that of a many-voiced animal. *"To the oars!"* cried the gunner, and suddenly everyone was working to move the yellow whaleboat out of range before the angry whale could strike.

The selkie watched with a mixture of fear and exhilaration. A single blow of the bowhead's tail could smash the boat to driftwood, and yet he was glad he had missed his shot, whatever it meant for him, or the crew.

The second whaleboat was moving in, hoping to correct the mistake made by the first, but the oars became snarled in the rope from the lance, and in the confusion and dismay, the whale passed under the two boats, and with a final heave, brought the flat of its tail crashing down, not on to the selkie's boat, but on the one that had come in to help, smashing the bows down into the wave and spilling the oarsmen like *skák tafl* pieces. Then it dived: more deeply this time, and the selkie heard its distant song, plaintive and eerie beneath the waves.

There was no time for the gunnerman to reprimand his son-in-law. The men in the water were seconds from death, and the crew of the surviving whaleboat were too preoccupied in saving lives and in salvaging equipment to comment on his failure. But the selkie knew from the sullen looks and hunched shoulders as they turned away from him that they had judged him wanting. A bowhead whale might have brought the men a hundred barrels of oil or more – a top-grade oil at six shillings a barrel; enough to earn them a tidy bonus, all of it lost along with the boat due to the selkie's carelessness.

"I'm sorry," he said to the gunnerman as they rowed back to the *Kraken*. "I must have been too hasty when I tried to take the shot."

The gunnerman said nothing. His eyes, as dark as the ocean, shone, and they rowed back in silence.

Four

The Captain had watched the incident from his place on the deck of the ship. Through his spyglass, he had seen the selkie miss his target; he had noted the gunnerman's rage and surprise, and the loss of the second whaleboat. None of this pleased him; and his face was dark as the men came back aboard.

Addressing the gunnerman, he said: "What went wrong?"

The gunnerman looked at the selkie, who waited for him to say that he had made a mistake born from inexperience; that he had overshot the mark in his eagerness to strike. But the gunnerman said nothing. Instead he looked out to sea, where the wreck of the second whaleboat was still afloat, in pieces on the spreading foam.

The Captain assumed a stern look. "I asked a question, McCraiceann."

Now the gunnerman looked at him. His eyes were dark and unreadable.

"I gave McGill the lance," he said. "I told him exactly where to strike. But instead of following orders, he aimed over the monster's head, and put men's lives at risk, as well as losing our chance at the whale, and a whaleboat, and all its equipment."

The Captain addressed the rest of the crew. "Is this a true account?" he said.

The men exchanged looks. "Aye, it is," said one.

"'Twas insubordination, you say?"

"Aye, sir."

"And do you all say so?"

"Aye, sir."

The Captain shrugged. "Then you know what to do. Fifty lashes, a night in the brig, and all his pay as forfeit."

And so they seized the selkie fast and stripped him to the waist, and lashed him to the *Kraken*'s mainmast, while the gunnerman fetched a knotted rope to carry out the punishment.

The selkie was puzzled and afraid. Why had the gunner not spoken for him? It would have been easy to say that, in the noise and confusion, there had simply been a mistake. But he had not done so. Why?

"You fool," said the gunnerman. His voice was barely a whisper, just loud enough for the selkie to catch without the other men hearing. "Why didn't you do as I said? Now you're to be flogged, or risk a worse fate from the rest of the crew." And, using the knotted rope, and to roars of approval from the men, he dealt out a summary justice that left the selkie bruised and bleeding.

After that they cut him loose and locked him in the *Kraken*'s brig; a cage, suspended from the stern and open to the elements. There they left him; shivering and raw as a newborn in the spray.

It was the longest night of his life. Everything hurt; his head was sore; his body felt grazed all over. And the *cold*, the dreadful cold that made him ache and hurt from within, as if every nerve were sobbing with a grief that could never be mended. And now the selkie understood that he would never be part of the whalers' clan; never again be respected, or welcomed into their community. There would be no more extra blankets, no more gunnerman's rations for him. He had squandered his chance – worse yet, he had put his crewmates at risk – and yet he felt no regret or shame for saving the bowhead whale.

"I would do it again," he said to himself, through chattering teeth. "I would do it ten times again. I would see every man on board drowned before I lifted a finger. Am I a monster? Surely, only a monster would betray his kind as I have done."

The brig was too small for him to move, or to take any kind of shelter, and so every time a wave hit the side he was lashed and stung and soaked to the skin with icy spray, until at last in his weakness and pain, he wept: and his tears fell through the bars of the cage and into the sea below him.

Five tears into the ocean.

Part 4

≈

"It was na weel," the maiden cried,
"It was na weel, indeed," quoth she,
"For the Great Silkie of Sule Skerrie
To hae come and aught a bairn to me!"

Child Ballad, no. 113

One

Meanwhile, the girl of the Grey Seal clan had followed the *Kraken* and watched its crew. She had seen the pilot whales; the basking sharks; the selkie's refusal to make a kill. Now she watched as he lay in the brig, abandoned by the gunnerman and all the rest of his human friends. And as the selkie's tears fell through the bars into the ocean, she responded to their call, as the selkie always do.

Leaving her sealskin to take human form, she looked up at the *Kraken*'s deck. The sea was very cold, and she shivered in her human skin, but her loyalty and concern for her friend gave her courage to go on. There was a watchman on the bows; but he looked slow and lazy. By keeping to the shadows, she thought she could avoid being seen.

She tied her sealskin to the stern of the ship, and, quickly and very quietly, climbed a trailing grapnel and made her way to the iron cage in which the selkie was imprisoned.

For a moment the selkie did not know whether he was awake or asleep. He saw a beautiful woman kneeling naked on the deck; the light from the moon through the clouds casting stripes of silver shadow on her skin. The woman's features were broad and strong: her hair as thick and dark as his own; and on her arms and belly he saw marks like his own tattoos; mystic spirals, curling waves; patterns like those on a sea-turtle's shell.

The woman put her hand to his lips to stop him from crying out in surprise. And then she put her mouth to his ear and sang to him in the voice of the sea, a voice that trembled a little with cold, and yet that he recognized at once:

> *We who once were kings and queens*
> *A-begging now we go*
> *Among the fields of ocean green*
> *And in the burning snow.*
>
> *In borrowed skin and borrowed clothes*
> *We frolic and make merry*

THE BLUE SALT ROAD

Beggars on the blue salt road
The salt road to Sule Skerry.

It was a song he had heard before, the song of the Grey Seal in his dream. But this time, he was wide awake, and he knew that the woman and the seal were one and the same; one of the selkie the gunnerman had told him were his enemies. But the beautiful woman did not look or sound like an enemy. She looked like *him*, he realized, and with a heavy slowness, like the tumblers of a giant lock falling into place, the selkie started to understand a part of what had been done to him.

"Do you know me?" he whispered.

The girl of the Grey Seal nodded.

"Are you from my *other* life, the one I have forgotten?"

She nodded again, and said to him: "But you did not forget it; rather, it was stolen from you." And whispering through chattering teeth she told him the tale of the sealskin, and how his wife had taken it, and with it all his memories of his clan and his life in the sea.

The selkie listened; first eagerly, with joy, and then in fierce and growing anger. He saw now how cruelly he had been tricked; how he had been made to eat of the flesh of the seal; and how close he had come to killing those who, in his true life, had been his friends. He saw how he had been made to be grateful to those who had enslaved him; how he had been taught to blame himself for his dislike of their customs; how he had been made to believe that his own people were monsters.

"Where is the sealskin?" he said at last.

"Your skin is kept in a cedar chest," whispered the girl of the Grey Seal clan. "Your wife keeps the key on a chain around her neck."

Then the selkie's mind went back to the day of his wedding: to the grandmother's warning, and to the song his mother-in-law had sung as she danced:

> *Three cheers for the bride and the bridegroom!*
> *Three cheers for the folk of the sea!*
> *And three cheers for the bridal chest,*
> *That was the maid's only dowry!*

Now it made sense, the selkie thought; the loss of his memory, the cold that would never leave him; his lack of appetite; his sense of disconnection with the world. And through all of it, Flora, her mother and the grandmother, watching him and smiling—

"They knew," the selkie said aloud. "Maiden, mother and crone, they *knew*!"

And with his anger there was shame, and sorrow, and a thirst for revenge. If he had been free, instead of locked inside the *Kraken*'s brig, in that moment he felt as if he could have slaughtered every man on board, and taken their skins, and drunk their blood until his thirst was satisfied. As it was, he pounded his fists against the bars of the brig, and barked and growled like a cornered seal, until the watchman on the bows called out angrily from his post: "Hold your tongue, or I'll silence it!"

The girl of the Grey Seal clan waited until the selkie had exhausted his rage. She was numb with cold now,

no longer shivering, but weak: and she knew there was no time to lose. She must regain her selkie skin, or die of the cold.

She whispered: "Please. Say nothing more. Let no-one suspect what you know. There is a lighthouse-man on Sule Skerry. Every three months he arranges for a ship to deliver provisions. This time, the *Kraken* will be making the delivery. Arrange to be among the crew of the boat. Try to speak with him alone."

"Why?" asked the selkie. "Is he one of us?"

The girl of the Grey Seal clan shook her head. "I cannot tell you more," she said. "His story is not mine to tell. But do as I say, and you may hear it. Till then, be humble, and bide your time, until your sealskin is back in your hands."

And with that, the Grey Seal girl left the ship and slipped back gratefully into her skin, leaving the selkie wide awake, and in a way that he had never been, not since the day he had found himself stranded on the lonely beach, naked and with no memory.

And next morning, when he returned to the crew, he spoke not a word to anyone, but was humble and obedient, so that even the canny gunnerman believed that he had learnt his lesson, and would cause him no further shame.

TWO

The days at sea passed slowly for the impatient selkie. Disgraced by his behaviour on the *Kraken*'s last whale-hunt he was spared from any further talk of becoming a gunner, but kept to his oar, like the other men, and was given no further attention.

This pleased the selkie, but the gunnerman made no secret of his bitter disappointment. A gunnerman's role carries status as well as a fatter pay-packet, and he had hoped his son-in-law would prove a worthy successor. The selkie's betrayal reflected upon the man who had vouched for him with the crew; and the gunner found that he, too, was shunned by those who had been his friends, and that his rations, his bedding and his privileges had also quietly been withdrawn.

As a result he barely spoke to his son-in-law, and the contempt in his eyes was clear.

This did not trouble the selkie at all: in fact, he scarcely noticed. Now he knew who and what he was, his hatred for the men on board the *Kraken* was even stronger than before, and his hatred for John McCraiceann was almost too much for him to bear. The other crewmen sensed this, and gave the selkie a wide berth, but they muttered behind his back that McGill was bad luck; a Jonah; a clocker who shirked his duties and brought malchance upon them all.

Certainly, there had been no more whales since his shameful episode, not even in the waters where the whale population was highest. The Captain promised to double the wage of any man who spotted a bow-head, a sperm or even just a pilot whale, but no-one did, and the *Kraken* sailed on with only a third of its barrels filled, and half its try-pots empty.

After three days of searching in vain, the Captain gave the command to sail north to a great deal of muttering among the crew, who had expected the haul to be greater and who saw their pay-packet dwindling with every day they spent at sea. They blamed the selkie for this, too – and with cause, for the Grey Seal girl had sent word to all the different whale clans to stay clear of those dangerous waters.

"Take heart," said the Captain. "There's still time for us to earn out our trip. There will be whales in the northern waters, and even if our bad luck endures we can fill the hold with sealskins on our way back home – for there will be seals aplenty once the warmer weather comes."

And so the *Kraken* journeyed north, and the girl of the Seal Clan followed it. She knew its destination: everyone knew Sule Skerry. There was a lighthouse built on the rock, run by a single man of the Folk; a man who had lived so long alongside the selkie that he scarcely knew to which race he belonged. This man had a reputation for being surly and anti-social, which made him an excellent lighthouse-man. It was said he had fled there many years ago, suffering from a broken heart, and had forsworn all company save for that of the sea-birds, the passing whales and, it was rumoured, the selkie. Whatever the reason, he never left the skerry, but had his provisions delivered to him, or traded with passing vessels for such luxuries as brandy and beer – as well as cheese and books, for which he had a voracious appetite.

The skerries were a well-known nesting-place for petrels, puffins and gannets, and there were colonies of seals and walruses that lived there mostly undisturbed. Whales and porpoises were plentiful, and the

shoals of herring shone like a miser's silver hoard. These things were all worth having, and the Captain meant to have as many as his crew could hunt.

But it was the whale that he coveted most – the bowhead and the sperm whale that lived beyond the skerries, and yielded the finest kind of oil, oil that was valued as highly as gold among the islands. The *Kraken*'s crew had intended to take as many of these whales as they could; to strip down the carcasses; take out the oil and store the barrels away below deck before returning home to sell them at the highest price they could. This had been the plan, at least until the selkie had lost them their second whaleboat, and now their chance of making a kill had been reduced by fifty per cent, and the Captain's face was grim as they sailed through the usually fruitful waters.

The crew, too, muttered in protest. "'Twas bad luck to take McGill," they said. "A man with no family, no clan; a stranger to our island ways. We should have known not to trust him. We should have thrown him overboard!"

The selkie said nothing, but bided his time, and thought of the songs of the Grey Seals, and of the tribe that he had left.

"When I have my sealskin," he thought to himself as he lay on his bed, "I will take back my son from the Folk, and teach him how to ride the wave, and swim with the dolphin and the whale, and hunt the bright shoals of herring. I shall teach my son to hate and mistrust the Folk that live on the land; and never to leave his selkie skin, except to do them mischief." He said this to himself every night, as the *Kraken* sailed further and further north, and his rage, which had been hot, grew cold and hard as mica. And day by day the *Kraken* sailed north, back into winter darkness; and the girl of the selkie followed it; and whatever followed after, followed silent and unseen.

Three

And now at last, the *Kraken* reached the outer skerries. Here it was colder than by the coast, and ice floated in the water. Further northwards, there was a mass of ice too thick for the *Kraken*'s hull to withstand, with walruses and sea-bears roaming the frozen wasteland. Here were islands alive with birds, where nothing grew but lichens and moss and great dark forests of floating weed. Here were kelps and furbelows and dabberlocks and purple claw; and buttonweeds and berry wart and pepper dulse and coxcombs. Here were marvellous caves of ice, where the voice of the winds sang strange harmonies. Here were colonies of seals, and porpoises, and puffins. And here were northlights that shimmered and shone throughout the long, long winter, like the billowing sails of a great bright ship that sailed across the heavens.

The *Kraken* dropped anchor by the sheltered side of Sule Skerry, where the lighthouse-man awaited his three-monthly cargo of brandy, beer, cheese and books. These, the Captain said, would be ferried to the shore by a team of four men in the whaling-boat; and payment taken in ivories – whale and walrus and narwhal – which the lighthouse-man had in abundance. No-one knew how he came by them: rumour had it that the lighthouse-man traded with the selkie, but no-one knew for certain. In fact, it was rare for the sailors even to see him. Most of the time they left his goods on a nearby spur of rock, then returned the next morning to collect their payment; for the lighthouse-man was known to be a recluse, and not at all fond of visitors.

The selkie had no trouble ensuring his place aboard the whaleboat. None of the men were in any haste to leave the comfort of their bunks, and when the Captain called for four volunteers to make the drop, all of them said: "Let them take McGill. If he falls overboard, it will be no loss to the rest of us."

The selkie pretended sullenness, but was well pleased to obey the command. Taking his place in the whaling-boat, he found himself flanked by the gunner-man, the Captain's Mate, and the crewman in charge of the ship's supplies. All of them were warmly-clad in thick coats, leather gloves, fur hats and boots lined with sealskin, but even so the selkie was colder than he had ever thought possible.

The rest of the crew had gladly remained, playing cards and keeping close to the warm try-pots of whale blubber from which the oil was extracted. But even without the promise of meeting with the lighthouse-man, the selkie was glad to leave the ship. Since he had spoken with the girl of the Grey Seal clan, the company of the other men had grown so oppressive that he longed to be ashore, even for a short time. And so he was glad of the task of helping with the delivery, and now he watched for the lighthouse-man with eager curiosity.

"We may not see him at all," said the Mate, when the selkie asked. "The lighthouse-man of Sule Skerry is a strange and complicated man. Not for nothing is he named *Sàmhach*, the *Quiet One*. He speaks little, smiles less, and seems to hate all of humankind almost as much as they hate him."

But when the crew of the whaleboat arrived by the little jetty between the rocks, they found the lighthouse-man already there: a tall and cheerless figure, clad in furs from head to foot, awaiting their arrival. There was a narrow sledge by his side, on which he meant to load his goods and drag them to the lighthouse.

The whaleboat pulled up to the jetty. The selkie leaped out to moor it. He allowed his wolfskin hood to fall away from his face as he did, giving the lighthouse-man a chance to observe his dark skin, his glossy black hair, his features, so very different from those of the other men on the whaler.

The lighthouse-man looked at him keenly. He seemed to be a man of late years, tall and strong and muscular, with long grey hair tied back beneath his hood of fur-lined oilskin. His face was hidden beneath a scarf, but his eyes were as dark as the sea, and as cold. For a moment his gaze fixed on the selkie, and then he spoke in a rusty voice, as if he were unused to everyday speech.

"My delivery?" he said.

"All here," said the Mate, indicating the boxes. "And our payment?"

"Here." The lighthouse-man gave a curt nod towards the walrus ivories strapped upon the wooden sledge. "Take them," he said, "But lend your man to drag the sledge back to the lighthouse. I'm not as young as I used to be, and the path is steep."

"Very well," said the Captain's Mate, with a gesture towards the selkie, who hastened to obey the command.

The lighthouse-man said to the selkie: "Follow me, and don't slip." Then he loaded the boxes onto the sledge, and the selkie prepared to drag them across the ice towards the lighthouse which stood on the rock, a finger raised against a sky oppressive as a bank of snow.

The warning was timely: the climb was steep and cobbled with patches of black ice. Underneath, there were lichens, and moss, and coral, and sea ivories that shone beneath the gleaming ice like the Moon Queen's treasure hoard. The lighthouse-keeper led the way; the selkie pulled the laden sledge, and finally both of them reached the highest part of the skerry.

Here, the lighthouse-man seemed to pause. For a moment he looked at the selkie. Then, he gave a little nod that served both as thanks and dismissal, and prepared to go back inside.

"Wait!" said the selkie.

The lighthouse-man turned.

"When we were by the jetty, it seemed to me that maybe you knew me. *Do* you know me, lighthouse-man? Have you seen my kind before?"

Once more, the selkie showed his face; his seal-

brown eyes, his jet-black hair. The lighthouse-man looked at him and shrugged.

"Aye, perhaps," he said at last. "Or perhaps you remind me of someone. Your name?"

"They call me *McGill*, the stranger's son. But it is no more my true name than *Sàmhach* is yours."

The lighthouse-man gave a thin smile. "No matter, son. Go back to your crewmates. You're young. You're strong. You have a wife, I'll wager?"

The selkie nodded.

"I did, once. A red-haired witch from the islands. Beautiful, and devious as only a girl of the Folk can be. But she betrayed me, and here I am, a traitor to my people."

The selkie became very still. "Go on."

But the lighthouse-man shook his head. "What does that old tale matter now? It was nearly a lifetime ago. What purpose does my knowledge serve, except to torment me? Go back to your woman, your life. Go back to your waking dream. I prefer my solitude, my rock, and the sound of the petrels."

But the selkie's heart had begun to beat very fast. "What knowledge?" he said. "What do you know? Who was the girl with the red hair? Where is she now?"

The lighthouse-man shrugged. "Who knows? That

was many years ago. I was young. I gave her a child: my child, whom I loved more than life itself. And my child was christened in the village church, in a robe of finest sealskin, and my woman gave it to me to hold, and I put my hands on the sealskin robe, and I remembered everything."

The lighthouse-keeper took a breath. "They say that the touch of his sealskin may release a selkie from bondage. My wife had cut mine into pieces to make a christening robe for the child, and only my memory was restored, with none of my former powers. And yet, from that moment I knew what my wife and her people had done to me. How they had lured me from my clan, and stolen away my memory. How they had made me betray my people and bound me into servitude. And now my child was theirs to keep, and was named and bound forever. And so I fled here, to my lonely rock, to live out my days in solitude among the seals and pilot whales, and herring gulls, and dolphins."

The selkie listened to all this with a heart that was pounding wildly. "My wife is with child," he said at last.

"Then pray you get home before the birth," replied the lighthouse-keeper. "Find your sealskin, wherever it is hid, and return to the selkie with the child. For the

babe must be given back to the Sea before it is christened by the Folk; otherwise it will never be free to
live with our clan in the ocean, but will belong to their
kind, wholly and forever."

The selkie stared at the lighthouse-man. "How can
this be?"

The lighthouse-man smiled; but there was nothing but misery and bitterness in it. "It is the way of
their women," he said. "Many's the time a girl of the
Folk has caught herself a husband, and had herself a
selkie child, to bring up alongside her kinsmen. But
captive selkie are never the same as when they were
wild. They yearn for the sea, they hear its voice even
though they have forgotten the tongue. They crave the
comradeship of a clan, even though theirs is lost to
them, and they seek out the company of men hoping,
perhaps without knowing it, to escape the tyranny of
women. And so their women, unsatisfied, look to the
comfort of motherhood, and claim their children for
the Folk before the selkie can take them."

"Then I must get back before May Day," said the
selkie, turning pale.

"That you must," said the lighthouse-man. "For
if your child is named by the Folk, he will never be
one of the clan, or hear the voice of the ocean, but will
grow up to be a gunnerman, and murder our people

for their skins, and die a beggar, when once we were the kings and queens of the blue salt road."

And at that, his tale told, the lighthouse-man went back into his tower, leaving the selkie to rejoin his crew, still thinking of the lighthouse-man's tale, and the beautiful woman who led him astray: a woman who would now be old, and with a red-haired child of her own—

But when he reached the shore where the whale-boat and its crew had been, he found both crew and boat gone, and the ship no more than a speck on the bright and beckoning horizon, with the green of the Northlights behind them like sails of phosphorescent silk. The crew had finally tired of the clocker in their midst; and, in the half-hour's interval between the loading of the lighthouse-man's sledge and his return to the jetty, the *Kraken,* the crew and the gunnerman had sailed away without him.

Four

The selkie stood for a long, long time, watching the distant horizon. The *Kraken*'s sail grew smaller and smaller against the veil of the Northlights, and the sky shifted green, to pink, to gold, and finally to deepest blue.

The selkie watched until the sky became a field of powdery stars, with the silvery blade of the crescent Moon reaping the clouds below them. Then, because he had no choice, and because he was aching with cold, he started once more on the path up to the Sule Skerry lighthouse. Knocking on the oaken door, he waited for the lighthouse-man: but when no answer came, he went in, and looked inside the building.

The lighthouse of Sule Skerry was built from blocks of gleaming grey granite. A spiral staircase led like a spine through several levels of habitation: a storage space: a living space: and finally, the great lantern, surrounded by mirrors, so that the room seemed to burn with cold fire. Here the lighthouse-man sat on a stool, his face no longer obscured by his hood, but clad in a knitted pullover over his sailcloth trousers. He was reading a book, although the selkie, having never learnt to read, could not make out the title.

"So, they left you behind," said the lighthouse-man, as he looked up and saw the selkie. His face in the lamplight was brown and strong-featured, with eyes that were inexpressibly sad, yet seemed to see so very far.

"I should have guessed," he said quietly. "The crew must have suspected you. Still, I suppose it could have been worse. They could have thrown you overboard. But sailors are superstitious. Maybe they feared the wrath of the sea. Or maybe they feared that the lighthouse-man, who keeps them safe from the rocks, would know what they had done to one of his own, and let their vessel go aground."

"I cannot stay here," said the selkie. "I must return to claim my child. Surely you have a boat – a fishing-boat, at the very least—"

The lighthouse-man shrugged. "Too late," he said. "I have only a small fishing-boat, made to carry me to and from my fishing-grounds and my lobster-pots. But even if I had a schooner, the *Kraken* has too much of a start, and will sail into harbour before you. The gunnerman, your father-in-law, will tell his tale to your woman, and she will cut up your sealskin, as my red-haired wife did mine, and baptize your child in the village church, and claim him for her people. This I have seen, and will see again – oh, many times, in my long, long life. It is my curse, my burden to bear, and now it will be yours, too."

The selkie shook his head fiercely. "There must be a way to follow," he said. "There must be a way off this skerry."

The lighthouse-man put down his book. His voice

was kind, but relentless. "There is no way," he said, "except by the boat that comes here every three months. By then, your child will be one of the Folk, never to swim with the selkie. Let him go; accept your fate; stay here on Sule Skerry. The life of a lighthouse-keeper is not without its consolations. I have a library of books, collected over my years on this rock. I can teach you how to read. I can teach you the language of the seals; the call of the puffin, the razorbill. I am old: one day the lighthouse will need the services of a younger man. You will take my place, in time. You can learn to be content."

"Never," said the selkie. "I will escape from this rock, or die." And, pulling on his wolfskin hood, he ran down the stairs, and out of the lighthouse to the shore, where the grey seals played, and stood by the half-frozen sea and called. But he had lost his memory, and along with it, the language of his folk, and the Grey Seals only heard the rage and harshness of his voice, and kept away, until at last, he fell silent, heartsick and despairing. Five tears in the ocean would have summoned them, but the selkie did not know this, and besides, his tears had been consumed in the blaze of his anger.

As for the girl of the selkie, she was unaware that her friend had been left behind on the skerry and she was miles out of earshot, still following the *Kraken*. The selkie called until his voice was as dry as driftwood, but no-one came; and when at last he turned away, he saw the lighthouse-man, watching him.

"I told you it was useless," he said. "Accept your fate, as I have done, and live out your life in exile."

Fiercely the selkie shook his head. "*I* may have lost my memory. But *you* have not. You can call them for me."

The lighthouse-man gave a sour smile. "Oh, I can call. But they do not always come to me, for I have damned myself with my foolishness."

"Try," said the selkie. "I beg you, try, so that my child and I can be spared your fate."

The lighthouse-man sighed. "Very well," he said. And, in the tongue of the Grey Seal clan, he began to call out for his people.

Five

It was a long and lonely call that rang against the frozen rocks like iron on an anvil. Over and over the lighthouse-man called, until the dawn began to break, cheerless over the cheerless sea. But when the first light skimmed the rock the girl of the selkie, who had heard the call and had understood what had happened, came to them in her Grey Seal guise, and looked at them with soft dark eyes. The selkie listened impatiently as the lighthouse-man spoke to her in the language of the seals, and then she was gone, with a flick of her tail, into the ice-grey water.

"Well?" said the selkie impatiently.

The lighthouse-man sighed. "She says there is a way," he said. "But I fear it will be dangerous. The blue salt road is a perilous one: frozen and filled with predators. Better to stay here, in safety, than risk your life for a forlorn hope."

"If there is hope, however forlorn," said the selkie, "I must try."

Once again, the lighthouse-man sighed. "Very well. I will pack as many supplies as I can into my tiny rowing-boat. I shall give you my warmest clothes, and oilskin bags to pack them in. Meet me here in an hour, and you will see the path that you have chosen."

The selkie did as he was bid, and an hour later, found his friend back where he had left him. Moored by the rocks was a small boat, laden with blankets and bottles and packages wrapped in pieces of oilskin. The boat's oars were neatly tucked away, and a long coil of hempen rope had been looped over the bow.

"Are you sure you want to do this?" asked the lighthouse-man. "I gave you all I could spare, but the journey will be dangerous. And if the boat overturns, the cold will kill you even before you drown, dragged down by the weight of your clothes."

But the selkie was not listening. Instead he looked at the angry sea, and the white-capped waves, and the floating ice, and beyond the ice, he saw the shape of a bowhead whale – a juvenile – that breached and breasted the soot-grey sea in a manner that he recognized.

"It is the whale whose life you spared," said the lighthouse-man to the selkie. "Today, she will repay the debt, and drag your boat as far as she can. After that, you must find your own way. May the gods of the salt road keep you."

And with that, the lighthouse-keeper turned and went back to his lighthouse; leaving the selkie alone with the whale and the rowing-boat, and the coil of rope. The selkie rowed out to the whale, looped a rope halter between her jaws, settled into the rowing-boat, and prepared himself for a sleigh-ride.

Part 5

≈

It shall come to pass on a summer's day,
When the sun shines hot on every stone,
That I shall take my little young son,
And teach him for to swim the foam.

Child Ballad, no. 113

One

The Folk have a name for the moment at which a harpooned whale tries to escape, dragging the whaleboat behind it. They call it a sleigh-ride, and so it seemed to the selkie in his boat; a wild and erratic sleigh-ride down the frozen blue salt road, all strewn with floating pieces of ice, each one capable of smashing the hull of the little boat like kindling.

The selkie had no means of steering, except by shifting his own weight from one side of the boat to the other, and the whale moved fast between the blocks of ice, leaving little time for him to knock them aside with one of the oars. Salt spray lashed his face; the green waves flung up frozen plumes.

The little boat skated and bounced along in the wake of the bowhead whale, sometimes balanced on its keel and sometimes tilting on its side, with the selkie holding on for dear life, and the waves rolling in all around him. His clothes were soon soaked through with spray; his hands, in their wolfskin gloves, ached with the cold, and still the sleigh-ride went on and on with the little boat lifting and pitching behind. The selkie was forced to accommodate as best he could until at last he became used to the rhythms, and found himself more in tune with the whale, anticipating its movements. His nostrils stung with dried salt, his hair was stiff with frozen spray, his fingers screamed with cold, and yet he was strangely happy, in spite of his fear and discomfort.

He realized that his silent friend was not entirely silent: above the perpetual crash of the waves came the melancholy sound of the whale singing to itself. And now, below the little boat, came the sound of other voices; some high, some low, swooping and soaring like strange birds. The rest of the whale clan were watching their child from the quiet, resonant deeps, their voices joining hers in a song as sad as it was beautiful.

Hours passed, the whale's progress slowed, and the selkie began to see a change in the ocean. The floating ice grew ever more scarce until it had vanished completely: instead, great barrel jellyfish moved through

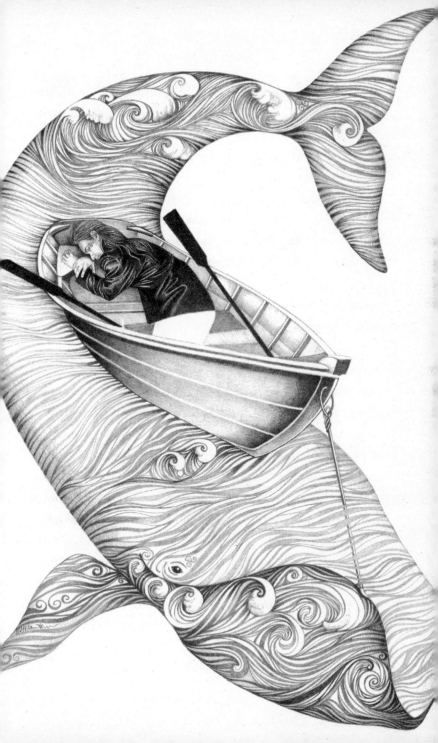

the clear dark water. These jellyfish were no obstacle: the slipstream of the boat moved them on, and they passed in his wake, majestic kings and queens of the Undersea, their soft and graceful bodies ripe and pale as summer peaches.

The selkie slept: and now that the ice was no danger, he dared to trust himself to the whale. Rolling himself in an oilskin under the sheltering stern of the boat, he let its movement take him, and in spite of the cold, he slept, and dreamed of the whales, and of the Undersea, and of the Grey Seals basking. And when he awoke, it was almost night: and the Northlights unfurled above him like a rainbow banner of dreams. The sea had calmed; the air was sweet and the stars came out in gleaming shoals. Below him, the selkie could still hear the singing of the bowhead whales, and as he moved, he seemed to sense the deeps of the ocean calling him in a voice he could almost recognize . . .

In a parcel in the bow of the boat, he found dried fish, black bread and cheese, and found himself suddenly hungry. He ate his fill, and drank some tea left for him in a flask by the lighthouse-man. Feeling warmer, he slept once more, and when he awoke it was morning.

Two

The following day was calm, and the whale had settled to a more leisurely pace. The little boat still rocked in its wake, but the sleigh-ride was over. The selkie sat under his oilskins, sheltering from the cold spray, ate more of the provisions left for him by the lighthouse-man, and found pleasure in the sounds of the sea: the rush of the wind; the splash of the waves, the distant song of the bowhead whales.

The sun came out from behind the clouds, and its light, though weak, was comforting. The year was beginning to turn at last; and with it, the long cold grip of the North had begun to loosen. A school of dolphins followed the boat, leaping and diving across the bows, scratching a trail of bubbles across the dark green of the ocean. There were great lion's-mane jellyfish as big as shaggy bales of hay, and small ones, that passed by invisibly, and shining phosphorescent ones that glowed like lanterns in the dark. There were shoals of silver herring and flocks of circling herring-gulls. There were pods of pilot whales, and great gentle basking sharks that glided by in silence. And always, on the rocks and skerries that marked the passage of the boat, there were colonies of seals – grey seals and spotted seals and common seals and harp seals – that nested on the weed-covered rocks or called and swam lazily in their wake. But whether these were the selkie's folk, or simply the everyday seals of the open sea, it was impossible to know, and the selkie felt a fierce and unexpected grief at the thought that he was so lost to himself that he did not even recognize his own people.

But there was *one* particular seal who seemed to follow as they moved south. A grey seal, a female with markings that seemed familiar. Was this the girl of the Grey Seal clan, who had come to him on the *Kraken*? There was no way to be certain, and yet the selkie believed it was, and was comforted by her presence. He began to look for her from his place in the boat, and called to her, though she never came close enough for him to see her properly.

On swam the whale, feeding on herring and mackerel as she moved through the warmer waters. As they travelled south the selkie began to feel a softening in the air; signs that spring was coming. The feeling brought him new hope; a certainty that he would be in time to save his newborn son, regain his true form and return to his clan. And so the days passed; and the little boat drew closer and closer to harbour.

And then, on the eighth day, when his supplies of food and drink were almost exhausted, the selkie saw a familiar shape on the blue horizon. A whaling sloop, with a fore-and-aft sail and a single topsail, it could have been any ship of the Folk; and yet the selkie knew what it was; knew and felt it in every nerve. It was the good ship *Kraken*, and as the selkie watched in dismay, he heard the familiar cry from the top of her single mast.

"Blooooooows!"

Three

The lookout had sighted the bowhead whale some moments before the selkie had seen the *Kraken*'s sail on the skyline. A young whale, moving in a fashion that suggested it might be injured, or sick – for a whale does not travel continuously on the surface of the waves. The lookout had seen the plume of white from the whale's twin blowholes, and now the selkie watched as the *Kraken* changed course, heading back in pursuit of them.

At once, he urged the whale onward. But he had forgotten the language of the creatures of the ocean, and his words meant nothing to her. She simply sang her mournful song as the *Kraken* came closer and closer, until at last, the selkie took his knife and cut the rope that connected the little boat to the whale, and

THE BLUE SALT ROAD

cried: "Go! Save yourself, before the whalers come for you!"

The whale must have understood the sound, if not the meaning of his words. For a moment she paused on the surface as the rope halter slipped from between her great jaws. For a moment the selkie saw her eye roll, softly and reproachfully; then she slid beneath the wave, her dark, stocky flank sinking soundlessly in a silver trail of bubbles. The little boat rocked to a standstill, and then was once more at one with the sea; drifting aimlessly with the waves, all its forward momentum lost.

The *Kraken* came closer; the selkie could see the faces of the men awaiting in readiness; he could smell the bubbling try-pots and the stench of death that clung to the ship. A week at sea had robbed him of his tolerance for that stench, and now he felt the familiar nausea sliding over him. As the whaler approached, he saw that the *Kraken* had launched its surviving whaleboat, and he saw John McCraiceann, the gunner, watching him from over the bow. The gunnerman's eyes were narrowed and dark beneath his woollen seaman's hat, and his face was grim as midwinter as he recognized the selkie.

"You should have stayed behind," he said. "You should have stayed with your own kind."

Joanne M. Harris

The selkie looked at him and smiled. It was not a pleasant smile, and the gunner recoiled from it. "My kind?"

The gunner exchanged glances with the rest of the crew. "You know what I'm talking about," he said. "I have to protect my daughter. I'll tell her you died bravely, at sea. No-one here will speak of her shame."

And at that he raised his whaling-lance and levelled it at the selkie.

"And what of your own?" the selkie replied. "What of *your* shame, gunnerman?"

During his time at sea, he had had time to consider the lighthouse-man's words, and those of the grand-

148

mother of the clan, and of the girl of the Grey Seal. The scattered pages of a book, a tale in a language he did not know, had finally come together to make a believable story. If he was wrong, then he would die – but his instincts, sharpened by the sea, told him that his suspicions were true, and he smiled once more at the gunnerman, who glared at him over the point of his lance and said: "I have no cause for shame, boy. I am proud of who I am."

"And who are you?" said the selkie. "Who was your father? What was his clan? And who named you John *McCraiceann*?"

"McCraiceann is an old island name," said the gunnerman steadily.

"And what does it mean, in the island tongue?"

John McCraiceann said nothing. But in his attempts to fit in with the Folk, the selkie had studied the many names of the clans, and John McCraiceann's name meant: *Son of the skin*. The gunnerman glared. "So what?" he said.

"Your wife must have been very beautiful, once," said the selkie quietly. "Red-haired, like her mother, was she? Red-haired, like her daughter?"

The gunnerman's face became very still.

"I'm sure you must remember that," went on the selkie softly. "Her red hair, her pale skin, so very different from yours. Do you remember, gunner-man? But what do you remember *before*?"

The gunner's face was still as stone, but the point of the whaling-lance trembled.

"What of *your* people, gunnerman?" the selkie went on relentlessly. "What of your mother and father? What of the McCraiceann clan? Surely you must remember *them*."

Slowly, the gunner shook his head.

"Tell me," said the selkie. "Did your wife ever have a cedar chest, with the key round her neck on a silver chain? Did you ever look inside, in all your years of marriage? And when your daughter came of age, did your wife give *her* the chest, as her mother did before her?"

Once more the gunner said nothing, although around him, his crew had grown restless. "Finish him," said one oarsman. "Don't let him bewitch you."

"Aye," agreed another. "Let him go back to the deeps, with the demons that do his will."

But the gunnerman did not move. His dark eyes held those of the selkie: beneath his anger, bewilder-ment.

"And what about your father-in-law? Did you ever know his name? Was it *Sàmhach*, the Silent?"

Slowly, the gunnerman shook his head but the point

of the lance began to drop. And now the selkie began to sing the song the girl of the Grey Seal had sung:

> *We who once were kings and queens*
> *A-begging now we go—*

To which the gunnerman gave a cry of terrible rage and anguish, and let fly the lance at the selkie, point-blank, with the bowline trailing—

Four

The selkie fell backwards, stunned by the blow. And yet the lance did not strike him, but instead went through the hull of his boat with a great, deafening, muffled report. The fishing-boat leaped on impact like a breaching whale, tossing what was left of his supplies and possessions overboard. The selkie fell into the water; and although these waters were warmer than those of the ice-bound skerries, he felt the shock immediately in the muscles of his chest; squeezing the air out of his lungs; dragging him under the surface.

He tried to struggle, but his clothes were already heavy with salt water. He shed his gloves and overcoat, attempted to kick off his boots, but already he was under the surface and sinking; hearing the sounds from the surface only as distant echoes. The voices of

152

the men on the boat were like ghost voices in a dream; the clang of the lance as it dragged against the hull of the fishing-boat like the ringing of distant bells. The sea was green and still and clear: a long strand of threadweed floated past, trailing silver bubbles, and the selkie was transfixed by the shape of its fronds, by its movements. He was suddenly certain that he could breathe underwater; that if he believed, then his selkie powers could somehow still return to him.

He took a deep breath, and choking, rose once more to the surface. The sea was no friend to him now, it seemed. Not in this human guise, at least. The sea was hostile territory; dragging him to a choking death. Then he felt a hand in his hair, dragging him towards the light, the sound, the cold, his enemies—

He struggled against the world above. Better to die cleanly, he thought, in the element that had birthed him. But then he heard the gunnerman's voice, whispering harsh and low in his ear: "Lie as still as a corpse," it said. "Unless you *really* want to die."

The selkie felt a stirring of hope. Had the gunner believed his tale? Had he recognized the song, the mention of the cedar chest?

He kept his eyes closed, feeling rough hands grabbing hold of him. A rope was looped under his arms, and then a life-belt of strips of cork. From the men on the whaleboat, he heard the sound of laughter.

"Let him drag behind the ship," said the voice of the gunnerman. "Let the sharks feed on his corpse. Let the demons of the sea be warned to stay well away from us."

He gave a bark of laughter, so that only the selkie heard when he whispered once more in his low voice: "Trust me, and do as I say."

The selkie did not struggle as the boat returned to the *Kraken*. He wanted to open his eyes, but dared not show any sign of life. The gunner's words suggested that he might have some kind of plan, and all the selkie could do was obey, and hope that his message had somehow struck home. And so he allowed himself to be dragged slowly through the water, and then, by listening to the voices on the deck above him, knew that his rope had been fastened to the *Kraken*'s anchor, dragging him in the wake of the ship like a lure for monsters.

Five

It was night when the gunnerman came quietly to release him. By then the selkie had ceased to feel the cold, and instead had begun to feel a kind of strange detachment, as if uncoupled from his body. He should have already been dead, he knew – no human could survive for so long in that freezing water – and yet he clung to life, as if somehow his selkie skills had not been completely forgotten.

Even so, the selkie was weak by the time the gunnerman came for him, his skin raw with long immersion in the water, and without the cork belt to keep him afloat he would certainly have drowned. But the gunner showed neither pleasure nor relief at finding him alive, merely pulled him from the water and led him to the try-pots still bubbling and boiling on deck,

155

and handed him a set of dry clothes – all in sombre silence.

"I volunteered for lookout," he said at last. "No-one will disturb us."

But when the selkie attempted to speak, the gunnerman silenced him angrily. "I saved you for my daughter's sake," he said in his harsh voice, "and for the sake of what we may share – I say only *may* —" he repeated, glaring at the selkie, "and because your tale raises questions for which I have no answers." He handed the selkie a piece of hard ship's biscuit and a flask of ale, and watched as the selkie ate and drank, his dark eyes never leaving his face.

"I have always loved the sea better than the land," he said, when the selkie had finished the food. "I have always loved the hunt, and the sound of the waves against the ship's hull. I have always loved the sting of the sea spray on my face. And if I am brown, it is because I have spent a lifetime in the open air. And if my memory is dim, it is because I am no longer young, and not because of some conspiracy. And as for the cedar chest, why, every girl in the islands has a chest in which she keeps her things. Flora's belonged to her mother, who had it from her own mother. So what?" He tried to sound scornful, and yet to the selkie McCraiceann sounded both bewildered and afraid. "Don't talk to me," he said. "Don't say a word. Don't even *look* at me, in case I decide to change my mind and throw you overboard instead."

And at that, the gunner opened the ship's hold, and pushed the selkie inside, and locked the hatch behind him. There would be food and water in there, as well as shelter against the sea; but the air was rank with the stench of death, and the barrels of whale-oil, and cured meat; and the selkie felt sick, and longed for the terrible journey to end. But there was nothing he could do to hasten the *Kraken*'s passage; and so he lay down and tried to sleep, and hoped to dream of the selkie. But all that night, and the following day, his dreams were dark and terrible: filled with the stench of fear and blood, and the sound of approaching thunder.

Part 6

≈

Then he has taken a purse of gold,
And he has laid it on her knee,
Saying: "Give to me my little young son,
And take thee up thy nourris fee".

Child Ballad, no. 113

One

Days passed, and the selkie continued to lie hidden in the *Kraken*'s hold. Outside, the air sweetened, in spite of the stench from the try-pots: spring was coming in at last, like an invading army. For the selkie, locked away from the light, forced to hide whenever the hatch was opened, it was a kind of torture. He had food enough for his needs and the hold was warm and sheltered, and yet he missed his fishing-boat, and the open sea, and the shoals of stars, and he sometimes thought he might go mad with longing for his freedom.

For three days he lingered, listening to the sounds from inside the whaling-ship: the voices of his companions from the sleeping-quarters; the sounds of activity from the deck. He knew the sound of every man's feet; he knew the creak of the braces that held the yards in place; the groan of the spars against the wind. And he knew the sounds of the hunt all too well; the cry of the lookout in the crow's nest, the sounds of the whaleboat being lowered, and he dreaded hearing these most of all.

And then, on the third day, the selkie heard the familiar call of the lookout-man. Surely not a whale, he thought – the *Kraken* had left those waters behind – but maybe something else; a shark, a colony of seals—

And now he remembered the Captain's words: *If our bad luck endures, we can fill the hold with sealskins on our way back home* – and he thought of the colonies of seals that lived around the islands, returning now with the warmer days to give birth to their fat cubs, and his heart turned cold at the memory, and at the idea of the slaughter to come.

Trembling, he went to the hatch that gave out onto the ship's deck. Through the hinges the selkie saw the crew preparing the whaling-boats for a hunt. The scent of the sea was stronger here, even over the stench of the hold, and the selkie's senses, enhanced no doubt by three days in the darkness, now seemed exquisitely attuned to every change and shift in the air, every movement of the waves. And now, through the crack in the door, the selkie thought that he could smell drying kelp, as well as the richer, darker scents of sea oak and buttonweed, and hear the barking of seals, and he knew that the *Kraken* was heading towards the ring of skerries that lay to the west of the islands.

Of course, the selkie could not *know* that this was the same ring of skerries that served as home to the Grey Seal Clan. But something in him sensed it nevertheless. Breathlessly, he listened to the familiar sounds of the preparation for the hunt: the winches that creaked as the whale-boat was lowered from its place on the deck: the voices of the crew; and above them, the voice of the Captain:

"Easy, boys, and spare no effort. I want three hundred skins today, and there'll be a keg of brandy for the man who takes the most!"

Three hundred skins. The selkie tried to imagine it. Three hundred slaughtered seals. Most of them cubs and females. Perhaps even the Grey Seal girl who had come to him on the deck. It could not be, he told himself. He had to stop them somehow. But how could he stop a whole crew? How could he fight off twenty men?

And then the selkie had an idea. Looking around him in the hold – the hold that should have been already filled with barrels of the finest oil, but was no more than a third full – he saw that his weapon had been here beside him all the time. The oil! The oil, which had been harvested from the flesh of pilot whales, and basking sharks, and porpoises – that oil would burn with a fierce flame, if only he could strike a light.

The selkie's keen eyes had become accustomed to the darkness. Now he searched through the ship's supplies and cargo for tinder and flint, or anything that would serve to light a fire.

At last he found it: a tinderbox, inside a case of lanterns. He worked to strike a flame – and then fed it with the tinder. When at last he had enough to set fire to some canvas, he made a torch, and, coughing from the smoke it made, set to lighting the barrels of oil, like beacons in the darkness.

Two

The oil caught quickly. A greasy smoke began to fill the burning hold. The selkie waited as long as he could for the fire to start to spread, and then he flung open the door of the hatch and hurled himself into the daylight.

For a time he was blinded by the sunlight on the sea. Everything in the world was white, as if the snows had come again. Shielding his eyes, he ran to the bow, and thought he saw the whaleboat, over-filled, some distance away, with the skerries in the distance. Almost all of the crew was on board. Every man was holding a lance, a harpoon, or a bludgeon. Of course, every man had hoped to be the one to win the brandy-keg. Only the Captain and his Mate remained on board the

165

Kraken – with two of the men, who clearly had drawn the short straw and had remained behind to handle the ship.

For a moment the crewmen stared, frozen, at the selkie. Smoke poured from the burning hatch. Somewhere in the reaches of the hold, a barrel of oil exploded.

Then at last, the Captain cried: *"Fire! Fire in the hold!"*

The crewmen and the Captain's Mate fled to bring water to the blaze. Fire is always a risk aboard a whaling-schooner, and there were hoses and buckets in place in case of such an accident. But it was too late: as soon as the water came into contact with the hot oil, the hatch exploded into flame, sending burning particles like rockets into the smoky air, spattering the burning deck, clawing the sails with yellow fire. It was as if the whales they had killed had been reborn into vengeful flame, spouting fire over the ship. The try-pots caught like paper lanterns. The sails were already burning. One man's hair was aflame, the other turned and jumped overboard. The Captain turned to the selkie, his eyes dancing with reflected fire.

"Demon," he said, and from his belt, he drew a long-barrelled pistol. *"Demon,"* he said again, and pulled the trigger – but either the breech had grown

too hot, or the powder ignited too soon in the super-heated air, for the pistol exploded in his hand, taking with it the hand itself as well as much of the Captain's face. What was left was unspeakable – and yet it kept screaming, a nightmare of blood and gleaming bone with the wall of fire at its back.

For a moment the selkie stared at the bloody, face-less thing, trying to summon the courage to put it out of its misery. Then, as the flames burned fiercer and the Captain fell forwards onto the deck, the selkie turned and jumped from the side and into the cold blue water below, and swam as fast as he could from the burning vessel. Meanwhile, the men in the whale-boat shouted and stared, and crossed themselves. All but the gunner, who stood in the bows in silent con-sternation.

The schooner was burning. The blackened sails shredded and turned into sheets of flame. The mast fell; staving in a deck that was already half-rotten with fire. The stench of burning whale-oil, of charred wood, of hair and flesh hung like a thundercloud overhead, bruising the air, tainting the sea, until at long last the vessel was nothing but a blackened hulk that sank slowly under the surface, leaving nothing behind but floating boards, charred wood, and pieces of wreck-age.

And through it all, the selkie watched from the nearby skerry: shivering in his wet clothes, his face as hard and still as the rocks on which he had taken shelter.

Three

By the time the crew had watched the last of the *Kraken* disappear: by the time the turbulence of its descent had abated, the sun – still a fleeting visitor to those northern parts – had sunk, and the skyline was corpse-green, with dark clouds riding in overhead.

The selkie was still sitting there, motionless on the weed-covered rock. Around him, in twos and threes, lay the seals, looking placid and unafraid. The *Kraken* was gone; the air had cleared, and the seals seemed to sense that the men in their yellow whale-boat were unable to do them harm. Sleek and fat, they stayed in their groups, keeping their cubs close, their brown and soulful eyes reflecting the carnage around them.

Sullenly, the crewmen stared at the selkie on his rock. Some murmured imprecations, but their voices were trembling. Surely the man was a demon, they said. Who but a demon could have enlisted the help of a whale to follow the ship? Who but a demon could have survived the treatment to which they had subjected him? Abandoned on Sule Skerry, then tied to the stern to be eaten by sharks, and yet, the hated clocker had managed not only to survive, but also to bring down the *Kraken*, the Captain, his Mate and the two crewmen who had remained on board. That meant demon magic, and although the crew were armed with lances and clubs, they raised not a weapon against him, but watched in fearful silence.

"This is because we threatened his folk," said one crewman to the rest.

"This is because we left him behind on Sule Skerry," another said.

"This is because we put him in the brig," said a third, and he held his weapon out over the bows, and dropped it silently into the sea.

One by one, the crewmen dropped their lances and cudgels overboard until only the gunner's lance remained, and he held it tightly to his chest, watching the selkie's face across the inky water. Then, in silence, he held out the lance and dropped it into the ocean. It made a splash, and the selkie thought he saw its fugitive gleam as it fell. He stood up from his place on the rock, and reached out his hand to the crewmen; and silently, without a word, the men on the yellow whale-boat lowered their oars and came to him, and made room for him to come aboard.

Then they raised the little sail and steered the boat east into the night, still without a single word to the selkie in their midst. They spoke to each other in lowered voices, and then only when necessary, with sideways looks at the selkie and not a word to the gunnerman. As far as the crew of the *Kraken* were concerned, John McCraiceann was a traitor, both to his kind and to the close-knit clan of his crew; and the contempt in their manner was clear, both to him and the selkie.

And so, throughout the night, they kept moving east, sometimes with the wind in the sail, sometimes working with the oars. Overhead, the stars came out; the sea was like a sheet of silk. They encountered no danger; no rocks; no storm; no fearsome monsters of the deeps. And when at last the dawn broke clear over the eastern horizon, they saw the land rising out of the sea, and knew that they were nearly home.

Part 7

≈

And thou shalt marry a gunnerman proud,
And a very proud gunner I'm sure he'll be,
And the very first shot that e'er he shoots,
He'll kill both my young son and me.

Child Ballad, no. 113

One

Spring in the islands is bittersweet: a brief and riotous flowering of harebell and heather, primrose and thorn. Sea pinks flower along the cliffs; cotton-grass in the marshlands. But the season is short; breaking out from the snows to die in the arms of summer.

Spring came in like a clap of thunder that year; wild and grey and simmering. The child in Flora's belly grew, and quickened and kicked imperiously. As the day of the *Kraken*'s return approached, Flora hoped that her man would be home in time to see the birth of his son – although her mother secretly hoped that the child would be safely christened by then.

"As soon as the child is born," she said, "make sure that he is named. A nameless infant summons the storm, and calls to the creatures of darkness."

What she *really* meant, of course, was that a child of the selkie cannot be reclaimed by its people once it has been christened. Her own mother had taught her this, on the day of Flora's birth; and with the baby almost due, the old woman had come over from the mainland to help with the delivery. Her granddaughter greeted her warmly enough, though secretly wondering how much she knew of the baby's father. But the old woman said nothing about selkies, or her son-in-law, but helped around the house, and cooked, and cleaned, and kept her counsel.

Meanwhile, Flora considered names for her son, so that she would be ready as soon as the child was delivered. Would he be *Arran*, the High One? Or *Fergus*, Man of Vigour? Or *Coinneach*, the Handsome? Or *Domhnall*, Ruler of the Worlds? Flora felt that her son's name should reflect his noble heritage; give the boy a sense of pride; do justice to her father's clan and the name of McCraiceann. It never occurred to her that the child would be anything but a son; and so, when on the first of the May, she gave birth to a healthy daughter, she was first surprised that her princeling had been born a princess, and then by the overwhelming surge of love she felt for the newborn infant.

Flora McCraiceann had never known love on any

other terms than her own. She had been fond of her parents, and yet had never felt close to them. Her lover, the selkie, had almost claimed a portion of her wild heart, but then she had tamed him to her will, and turned him into something else; a household pet, for whom she had learnt to feel affection, nothing more. But now came motherhood; and for the first time, Flora McCraiceann was in love. From the tip of her nose to her rust-red curls, the newborn infant was wilful and wild: one day refusing to suckle, the next, screaming for her mother's breast.

"A difficult child," said the mother. "She will be easier after the christening." But Flora loved her daughter wholly and unconditionally, and did not want to see her change, not even for her own comfort. Perhaps this was why she did not take the child to be christened: or perhaps she was waiting for the *Kraken*'s return; but, whatever the reason, her daughter was still nameless when the yellow whaling-boat sailed into the harbour.

The men aboard had been sailing for forty-eight hours. They were hungry, and thirsty, and cold, and afraid – all but the selkie, whose silent presence had kept them equally silent. Now, as they reached their journey's end with their lives as their only bounty, they started to whisper once again, remembering the barrels of oil, the skins and ivories on board their ship, all lost to the selkie's dark magic. John McCraiceann also looked bleak, and he perhaps had more reason: after all, he had saved the selkie from drowning, and brought him aboard the *Kraken*. The crew had taken little time in coming to this conclusion, and now that they were almost home, at last they were emboldened to speak against their former friend and his son-in-law.

"McCraiceann brought the clocker on board," said one. "He brought misfortune onto the ship."

"He owes us all," said another. "Every crewman's wages lost, for the sake of one man."

"*If* he's a man at all," said a third, forking the sign against the evil eye slyly with his fingers. But the crewmen, in spite of their mutterings, dared not face the enemy, but turned away, their faces grim, and would not look at them at all. But the tale would spread, the gunnerman knew, and soon the whole island would know he had sided against his crewmates for the sake of an outsider.

"This will be the end of me here," he said to the selkie as they walked home. "No-one will buy goods from my wife when she goes to market. My daughter will be shunned in church. What have I done to my family, to the life I worked so hard to build?

Why did I listen to you and your tale to frighten children?"

"You listened because you knew it was true," replied the selkie. "In your heart, you always knew that you were a child of the ocean."

The gunnerman shook his head stubbornly. "I loved the whaler's life," he said. "That doesn't make me one of you."

"So, you admit you know what I am?"

"A madman," said the gunnerman. "A madman and a murderer." But he would not meet the selkie's eyes, and his voice was rough and low.

"What of the cedar chest, and the key?"

"What of it?" said the gunnerman. "All women have a linen chest. Your story proves nothing. I trust my wife."

"Then show me I'm wrong," said the selkie. "Look inside the cedar chest. Find the sealskin hidden inside. Touch it once, and your memory will return. You will know how they cheated you: how they stole your life, your child – for Flora would have been one of us, if you had but claimed her. And now my child may meet the same fate—"

The gunnerman gave a low growl. "Enough," he said. "I shall look into the chest. And what I find there will decide – if anything – what I will do." And with that he lapsed into a sullen silence, from which noth-ing the selkie said would rouse him. And so they took the long road home from the island harbour: and came to the house on top of the cliff to the sound of church bells ringing.

TWO

For the selkie, it had been a long and strange adventure. His time aboard the *Kraken* had been hard, and his return ever harder. Now within reach of his home again, he found himself almost hoping he was wrong, that Flora was blameless, that none of his convictions were true.

The lighthouse-keeper had been half-mad with anger, grief and solitude. The tale that had made sense at sea, among the seals and skerries, now seemed outlandish, even to him, now that he was back on dry land. There were no selkies. The Grey Seal girl was a dream, born from desperation. He had been in no rational state the night she had come to him on the deck. Freezing cold and in distress, he could easily have imagined her.

The selkie had almost convinced himself when he reached the gunner's house, surrounded now with spring flowers. Sea pinks; purple campion; iris, oxeye daisies, with yellow gorse and primrose and vetch growing along the cliffside path. The selkie had never seen so much colour all in one place; and when the door opened and Flora came out, all in white, just as she had been on their wedding-day, his time on the *Kraken* seemed little more than a nightmare.

Behind her, came his mother-in-law; and her mother behind her, both of them in their finest gowns, their hair dressed under caps of lace. The old woman was all in black; her daughter all in grey, and Flora in white, with a child in her arms, a newborn in a sealskin sling, wearing a long linen robe—

Flora had finally succumbed to her mother's entreaties and agreed to have her daughter named. Without mentioning the selkie, or referring openly to his circumstances, she had still managed to sow the seeds of doubt in her daughter's mind.

"A nameless child can never be safe," she had said to Flora. "A nameless child is easy prey for the hungry Travelling Folk. They will claim her, and steal her away, and you will never see her again."

Little by little, Flora had come to accept that a christening was the only way to keep her daughter safe from harm. And now that the selkie had returned, she realized she had delayed too long, and she held her child close, and promised herself that no-one – not the selkie, nor the Grey Seal clan, nor even Lord Death himself – would rob her of the little one she loved more than anything else in the world.

And so she smiled at the selkie, although her heart was pounding in fear, and said: "See! We have a daughter, my love. The image of her father. What do you think of *Gormlaith*, Princess? Or maybe *Moire*, Star of the Sea?"

For a moment the selkie's blood froze. He looked at the child in Flora's arms. That robe, all embroidered and hemmed with lace – could that be a christening robe? And the sound of bells from the village church—

"Am I too late?" the selkie cried. "Am I too late for the christening?"

Flora smiled at him again. "Of course not," she said. "I knew you were coming back today. I heard it from a waggoner coming from the harbour. I was so glad you could be here to help name our lovely daughter."

And in that moment Flora McGill almost believed her own words. The thought of being a family – which was all she had ever dreamed of – now overrode her suspicion and the fears that her mother had awakened in her. She looked at the selkie, her husband, and she thought she saw something in his eyes – a wildness, like that of the ocean – and felt an old fire rekindle in her, a fire she had thought forever extinguished.

The selkie thought that, in that moment, Flora had never looked more beautiful. Once more, he was tempted to say nothing of what he had learnt, but to slip back into his life with her like a drowning man into a wave, and surrender himself to ignorance. He had a home; a beautiful wife; a family ready to welcome him. He could be happy; he told himself – and if not happy, at least content.

But then he looked at his newborn child, warmly-wrapped in her sealskin sling – and the old, familiar nausea slid over him like a fever. To wrap up the child in a sealskin seemed to him monstrous, obscene; and suddenly he was convinced that it was his *own* skin swaddling the infant, and he reached out with trembling hands to touch the soft fur with his fingers—

But the sealskin of the baby's sling was just an ordinary skin. There was no return of memory; no sudden revelation. The selkie was both relieved at this and oddly disappointed. If only he could be *sure*, he thought; if only this fear could be laid to rest. If only he could look in the chest, and find the sealskin hidden there—

But Flora was wearing the silver key around her neck like a talisman, and now the selkie realized that the mother and the grandmother wore identical silver keys, which gleamed from the lace around their throats – the grandmother's on a piece of black lace, the mother's on a fine grey cord. There was no way he could take a key without arousing suspicion. And yet the cedar chest contained the answers to all his questions. Without it, he could not risk trying to disrupt the christening. And what if he was wrong, he thought? What if the Grey Seal girl had lied? What if there was no sealskin there, and he had just imagined it all?

Finally he said to his wife: "We are weary and travel-stained. Give us time to change our clothes, and we will join you for the ceremony."

Flora looked at him closely. "Very well, my dear," she said. "Meet us at the church, and we will celebrate together."

Meanwhile, the gunner's wife was showing signs of impatience. She was eager to christen the child, and safeguard her future among the Folk. But news travels fast on an island, and the tale of the *Kraken*'s crew had already reached her. It was not an entirely new tale, and the gunnerman's wife had quickly understood that her husband and son-in-law were in danger of learning the truth. She knew that they meant to look in the chest as soon as she and Flora were gone; and she feared for the life she had built for herself, and for her new-born grandchild.

But then she thought of the grandmother. If the old lady stayed behind, then surely the chest would be safe, she thought. In any case, the grandmother could keep the men talking until the christening was done – which was, after all, the main concern. Men of the selkie were easy enough to come by, thought the gunnerman's wife; but to lose her grandchild now would be a terrible loss to the family. And so she signalled the grandmother to stay behind and watch the men, and hurried with her daughter to the little church on the cliffside, where the Parson was waiting for the child, to claim her forever on behalf of the Folk.

Three

The selkie and the gunnerman were left in the grand-mother's company. The old woman looked at them mockingly, as they exchanged helpless glances.

"Aye," she said in her cracked voice. "So many difficult choices to make! A white shirt or a black one? A sealskin cap, or hatless? Men are vain, so very vain. Especially the men of the sea. Vain and easily led, I fear: and so turns the world, and always will."

The selkie looked at her and smiled. "There's only one choice, Old Mother," he said. "Give me the silver key you keep on the chain around your neck, and give me back my sealskin."

The old woman laughed. "Too late," she said. "I tried to warn you. They don't call it 'wedlock' for nothing, I said. And yet you walked into the trap. I knew a man like you, once. Handsome, and stubborn, and reckless, and proud. He gave me a child – a daughter – but he did not stay to watch her grow. The men of the sea have always been faithless in the end. And that is why we take what we can, and keep our little secrets, for what else can a woman do in a man's world, ruled by a man's laws?"

The selkie said: "You stole his life."

"And what would he have left of mine?" said the old woman fiercely. "A *nourris* – a wet-nurse – that's all I was to him and to his people. He would have taken my daughter away, and given her to the Folk of the Sea. Maybe he would have paid me in gold, as the Sea-Folk are wont to do. And I would not have recognized her skin among the many piled up on the traders' stalls on festival and market-days." The old woman lifted her chin, and her eyes were ablaze with sudden rage. "You men," she said. "You're all the same. Men of the land, or men of the sea. You take everything a woman can give – her maidenhead, her love, her child – and still you want your *freedom*—"

The selkie flinched at the sting of her words, and yet he held her furious gaze. "Give me the key, old woman," he said. "Before I decide to take it."

"Aye, that was always a man's way," she said. "Take it, then. Much joy may it bring. But heed my words,

Man of the Sea: some things are better left unremembered." And she reached for the lace around her neck and gave the selkie the silver key, though her eyes shone with rage as she followed him into the empty house, with the gunnerman following after them, and up the stairs to the cedar chest which held so many secrets.

Four

The chest was old and darkened with age, but still smelt faintly of cedarwood; and there were sachets of lavender stitched into the lining. Inside they found Flora's wedding-gown, made from the white skins of baby seals, and beneath it her mother's, of heavy satin trimmed with fur, and beneath that, a wedding-gown so old that the lace had grown brittle as autumn leaves, the silk like Bible pages.

The grandmother sat in a rocking-chair beside the chest, and watched them, and rocked. "That was *my* wedding-gown," she said. "It may seem like a hundred years ago that I was a bride, and yet a bride I once was, and happy enough, until my man betrayed me."

"He did not betray you," the selkie said. "The truth was too much for him to bear."

The old woman shrugged. "He had a choice. As both of you now have a choice: keep your lives, or throw them away. Each of you has a wife here. Each of you has a daughter. Will you sacrifice them now for the sake of foolish pride?"

But the selkie would not listen to her. He emptied the cedar chest of every piece of linen therein: wedding-dresses, tablecloths; embroidered napkins; underthings. And there, at the very bottom, he found a parcel of tissue-paper: and inside the tissue-paper, a skin, a sealskin soft as a summer's day; a skin as grey as mist on the sea. Eagerly he pulled it out; but once more there was nothing. No revelation, no memories. The lovely skin was not his own. But then, the gunner-man put out his hand and gently touched the soft grey fur—

The grandmother smiled. "I warned you," she said.

John McCraiceann clutched the skin and staggered backwards, breathing hard. He looked like a man in the throes of some unimaginable pain, or some undreamt-of ecstasy. He tried to speak, but could not: tried to turn, but could not; looked up at the old woman, then fell to his knees beside the chest and began to weep in great, thick, sobs. The selkie looked into the chest in search of a second sealskin; but there was nothing left inside, except for a few dried lavender-heads and a single handkerchief.

The grandmother smiled and rocked in her chair. "My daughter was sentimental," she said. "She used to wrap herself up in that skin when her husband went to sea. I told her many times that she should cut it up, as I did mine, to make sure her husband did not stray, but she was always a stubborn thing, and thought she knew better than I did."

"Old Mother. Where is *my* sealskin?" said the selkie, trembling.

"Who knows?" replied the old woman. "My daughter is a poor seamstress. She never knew how to make the best of a selkie skin. My Flora, on the other hand—"

The selkie took a sharp breath. "Where is it?" he cried. "What has she done with my sealskin?"

But there was no answer to his cry. The grandmother watched in silence and rocked, and the gunnerman was still beyond speech, as the memories came tumbling down upon him. For thirty years he had lived with the Folk. Thirty years of hunting his own; thirty years of eating their flesh. He wrapped himself in the sealskin and wept for all that he had done to his kind; for the joy he had taken in hunting them; for all his

193

years of ignorance, and for the end of his thirty years of peaceful marriage, fond fatherhood, and joy in being the provider for his little family—

The grandmother watched him with pity and resignation. "I warned you from the first," she said. "I said no good would come of this." Then, to the selkie, she went on: "See what we have spared you? A selkie who betrays his kind cannot hope for forgiveness. And a man who betrays his family cannot hope to be taken back. What remains for such a man? Where will he go, when rejected by all? But there is still hope for you. For you, there is the chance of a life. Will you take it?"

But the selkie only repeated: "Old Mother, where is my sealskin?"

The grandmother shrugged. "You men," she said. "All of you so foolish and proud. What good can it do to know that now? Think of your child, man of the sea. Think of the life you want for her. Will you give her a loving family to care for her, or will you give her a broken home, an absent father, a mother alone?"

For the third time, the selkie replied: "Old Mother, where is my sealskin?"

The old woman sighed, and shook her head at his stubbornness. "In silver were you bound," she said. "In silver, lies the thing you seek."

"Silver?" said the selkie. "If not the silver key to the chest, then what kind of silver do you mean?" And when the old woman would not reply, he began to search the house; flinging open wardrobes and drawers, turning out kitchen cupboards for every piece of silverware in search for a clue to the riddle.

But the gunnerman's house was poor. There was no silver to be found, except for a few little trinkets on Flora's dressing-table.

"What does it *mean*?" said the selkie, turning at last to the grandmother. "Tell me, or I'll wring your neck!"

The old woman watched him and rocked in her chair, her dark eyes shining maliciously. "'Tis not the wringing of my neck, but that of the church bells you should mind," she said, and suddenly the selkie saw how the old woman had lured them; how she had kept him talking while the others carried the baby to church. How much time had he wasted? Was he too late for the christening?

The old woman cackled and rocked in her chair. "Which one will ye choose?" she said. "The sealskin or the christening? Your life, or that of your daughter?"

But the selkie had already started down the stairs towards the door. He took the cliffside path at a run, the grandmother's laughter following him.

"In silver it lies!" she cackled again. "In silver, your salvation!" But there was no-one to hear her now, except for the weeping gunnerman, as the selkie ran towards the church, where the bells were already ringing.

Five

The church was a small stone building with a single wooden spire. The windows were narrow; the coloured glass allowed little light to enter. Instead there were candles everywhere, filling the hall with a soft glow. It shone on the silver vessels that were lined on the altar, and on the faces of the Folk gathered in the pews (although there were not many guests: the news of the *Kraken*'s loss had already reached the small community).

Flora, in white, her mother, in grey, and the Parson, all in black, were standing by the marble font. The child was asleep in her mother's arms, the christening-cap discarded, and in that moment the selkie was sure that he was too late; that the child had been named.

But then he saw his mother-in-law's face, the sudden

sharpness in her eyes, and hope bloomed again inside him. Summoning every shred of control, he smiled at the mother-in-law and said: "I hope I'm in time for the ceremony?"

Flora gave him a questioning look. "You haven't changed your clothes," she said.

"Forgive me: I was impatient to be here."

"My husband?" said the mother-in-law.

"He's only a moment behind me."

The mother-in-law glanced at Flora. Both women looked uneasy. But the Parson, who had heard nothing of the events on board the whaler, smiled and said:

"Of course we must wait for McCraiceann. How could we let him miss his only granddaughter's christening?"

The selkie kept an outward calm, although his heart was beating fast, and tried to feign interest in the words of the Parson, who, sensing none of the tension in the folk around him, babbled on benignly:

"The McCraiceanns were always good friends of the church. I christened Flora myself, you know – it seems like only yesterday – and such a pretty child she was, with her mother's red hair and her father's dark eyes. A little wild, perhaps, at first, and yet she has grown so accomplished! Why, just the other day, she presented us with an altarpiece. The most marvellous work – her grandmother's idea, I believe – and fine enough, I swear, to adorn the greatest cathedral in the land—"

At this, the selkie saw his wife flinch. His eyes went to the altar, gleaming with polished silverware. And underneath the silverware – the paten and the candlesticks, the chalice and the monstrance – he saw a finely-worked altarpiece that seemed to be made of animal skin—

In silver, lies the thing you seek.

He made a lunge for the altar.

"No!" cried Flora.

But it was too late; the silverware had fallen, crashing, to the floor, and the altarpiece, with all its fine work, with all its chasing in silver thread, with all its silken embroidery, was in his hands. As soon as he touched it, the selkie knew without a doubt that this was *his* skin; shaved and embroidered and painted and stamped and made into an ornament for church-going Folk to marvel at, and he gave such a cry of pain and despair that Flora and her mother grew pale, and the infant began to cry.

"Flora, what have you done?" he said.

"Coigreach, please," said Flora.

"That's not my name!" cried the selkie, and in his rage kicked over the font, which smashed on the

pavement in front of them as all his stolen memories came rushing in again like the tide. How easily they had duped him, he saw. How compliant he had been! For three generations, and doubtless more, the red-haired women of the islands had enslaved the men of the selkie. The lighthouse-man, the gunnerman, and finally the selkie himself—

He flung the sealskin onto the ground, hoping to stop the memories. But there was nothing he could do: the sealskin was ruined, its power gone; and he was doomed to remain on land, and remember the sea, forever.

Six

And now he remembered everything: the voice of the ocean; its languages; its rhythms and its changing moods. He remembered the songs of the Grey Seal clan; the sound of the waves on the skerry. He remembered the taste of redfish, caught between his snapping jaws; the sweetness of shrimp, and the richness of cod, and the salty crunch of green urchins. He remembered the song of the minke whale; the dance of the ghost crab on the shore, the cry of the curlew on the tide, and his heart ached with grief and happiness.

Now he remembered his old friends; the Grey Seal girl, his playmates; his mother, the matriarch of the clan who had warned him against the Folk, and all his lovers and siblings. He remembered his first steps as a man, and the joy he had felt in shedding his skin.

He remembered the excitement of spying on the Folk of the land, and the way he had followed their fishing-boats, listening to their voices. But most of all he remembered the red-haired girl on the moonlit beach, and the waves, and the warm wind blowing, and he was filled with sorrow for the brief, sweet story they had shared.

And finally, the cruellest of all the demons in the box, came love: the taste of her salt skin, the feel of her hair, the touch of her hand, her laughter under the silent stars. The feelings that had disappeared when the selkie lost his memory now returned like the rising tide, tainted with bitterness and the knowledge of her betrayal.

He turned back to Flora. "*Why*?" he said. "Why did you do it, Flora?"

Flora's eyes were brimming with tears, and yet she looked hard as granite. "Because my grandmother taught me well. Because you men are all the same. I thought that perhaps you were different, that I could keep you faithful to me, but you had to return to the sea, didn't you? The cruel sea, that sings so sweet, even through a lover's embrace. Women are nothing but vessels to you, cheap and easily broken. I wanted something of my own, something no-one would take away."

A murmur arose from the Folk in the pews.

"You used me," said the selkie.

"I *saved* you. You were a savage," she said. "Look how far you have already come!"

"I have betrayed my people," he said. "*Our* people: yours and mine." And he told her the tale of the gunnerman, and then the tale of the lighthouse-man; and Flora's eyes grew, first wide, then hard as fragments of mica.

"There's none of your blood in me," she said. "My mother and I are true islanders." But her mother looked away, and bit her lip, and would not look at her again, and the Parson, in consternation, tried to silence the folk in the pews as their voices grew loud and harsh.

"Your father was from the Grey Seal clan," went on the selkie relentlessly. "Your mother trapped him, as did her mother before her. You are both daughters of the sea, robbed of your inheritance. But this child is of the Grey Seal clan, and now for my clan, I claim her."

Flora shook her head and wept. "I will not let her go," she said. She turned to the Parson, pleading: "Name her, Parson, keep her safe!"

"I cannot," said the Parson. "Not when her father has claimed her."

Flora held the child and wept. "He cannot!" she said. "He cannot return! Not without his sealskin! How can he claim her for the sea, when he cannot raise her there?"

It was true; the selkie thought. What use was his knowledge of the sea if he could never return to his folk? How could he teach his child their ways? How could he protect her?

Flora, sensing victory, raised her chin defiantly. "You see?" she said. "She belongs with me. She belongs with those who love her. The Folk of the Sea do not need her, but I do. *I* do!"

And then, from the door, there came a voice: the quiet voice of the gunnerman. His face was raw with tears, but his eyes were clear and full of knowledge. Under his arm, he was carrying the sealskin from the cedar chest.

"And what of the child? What of *her* needs?" he said.

Flora clutched the infant fiercely in its sealskin sling. "She needs her mother, her family. She needs the love and security that only I can give her."

The gunnerman smiled. His eyes were sad, but his voice was unexpectedly strong. "I understand, my daughter," he said. "For the first time in years, I understand. But would you have your child as she *is*, or make of her a tamed thing, as you tamed her father?"

"I'll not have her brought up by savages! I'll not have her forget me, and leave me alone with nothing!"

Once more the selkie looked at his wife and wondered at the wildness in her. She might have been claimed by the Folk, he thought, but he now realized that he could see much of the Grey Seal clan in her, too. The passion that had called him to her from the depths of the ocean: the passion that had made this child burned in her like wildfire. And the selkie was still drawn to that fire, even though it had burnt him once, but knew not how to reconcile the call of it with the call of the sea.

"How can I choose?" he said to himself. "How can I take our child away? But how can I leave her here on land, knowing everything I know?"

Finally the gunnerman spoke. "Let *me* take the child," he said. "Let me teach her the ways of the sea, as I should have taught *my* daughter. For one year, she will live in the sea, and for one year, she will live on the land; and then return to the sea again, and then return to the land; and so for all her life will be a child of both, bound by neither."

For a long time Flora said nothing. Then she looked

at the selkie. "And will *you* stay, and bring up your child? Or will you leave, as men always do?"

The selkie looked at the gunnerman. It was a solution, he told himself. Not the solution for which he had hoped; but at least, this way he would have the chance to see his daughter flourish and grow. But what of his wife? She had lied to him; and yet he remembered loving her once. Could he love her again? He did not know, though he thought she looked somehow different now. Something in the eyes, perhaps; a new kind of light; a softness.

Finally, he held out his hand. "One year with the Seal Folk," he said. "One year with us, on land. I shall stay, if only to be sure that the Land Folk keep their word, and do not try to steal her away, or feed her the flesh of her people. Will you give me your promise?"

For a moment Flora looked at him. Then she took his hand. "I will. Will you give me yours?"

"I will."

The last time the selkie had left that church was when he had married Flora. This time he left it a changed man, acting of his own free will, holding his child in her christening robe, with his wife beside him.

For a moment he paused by the oaken door. Then, turning to Flora, said: "Moire. *Star of the Sea*. A good name."

"Very well," Flora said. "Moire shall be our daughter's name." Then, drying her eyes, with head held high, she followed the selkie out of the church and into the warm spring sunlight. The guests all left in silence, and the Parson picked up his silverware and put it back onto the altar. And, then together, the family went down the cliff to the sandy beach where long ago Flora and her man had lain in the moonlight and laughed, and loved. There, the gunnerman took the child and slipped into his sealskin, and then, as a Grey Seal, swam away, with the child as a white pup beside him.

The selkie and Flora stood in the surf and watched until the two Grey Seals had vanished into the distance. For a time they heard them still, barking over the sound of the wind. And then, when they were long gone, the selkie once more took Flora's hand, and together they walked back up the path towards whatever the future might bring.

Epilogue

The ocean has so many stories to tell. Stories of the McCraiceann clan that live in the westernmost skerries: stories of the bowhead whale, who always remembers a kindness; and stories of *Moire*, Star of the Sea; the child of two different fathers, who swims with the seal, and sings with the whale, and sometimes hunts the whalers themselves on their journey northwards.

This is such a story. Told to me by a gunnerman, who was once a man of the Folk, before he became my father. Told to me by a man of the Folk, who was once a man of the Grey Seal clan, before he too, was my father. Told me by a lighthouse-man, living alone with his memories, keeping all his stories between the pages of his many books. Told me by my mother, who greets me every twelvemonth with tears, and talk, and love, and laughter. Told me by my grandmother, who sits in her rocking-chair, watching the sea; and by *her* mother, so old and white that she might almost be cobwebs, except for her eyes, which are dark as the sea, and filled with unspoken memories. This is her story, too: a story of fear, and suspicion, and love, and men and women, and daughters, and sons, and all the dark spaces in between. This is the story of every man who ever felt trapped by a woman's love; the story of every woman who feared the tyranny of her fathers.

And this is *my* story; a story of change, betrayal, and forgiveness. But most of all, of love – between a man and a woman; a parent and child; or the love of a creature for their world. Take from it what you most need, and pass it on to someone else, for this is how we all move on; changing, unchanging, like the tides, taking with us what we can, and scattering tales to the four winds, like seeds upon the ocean. For sixteen summers I have lived, half on the land, and half in the sea, and from my father I have learnt the stories of the Grey Seal clan, and how to elude the seal-hunters, and how to hear the songs of the sea, and how to ride a bowhead whale. From my mother I have learnt the tales and legends of the Folk, and how to sew, and how to spin, and how to harness the power of tears.

My name is a curse to those who live by hunting the lords of the ocean, and a blessing to the fishermen who follow the silver darlings. For I am Moire, Star of the Sea, named among the nameless. And I am as free as the moonlight, and wild as the crashing of waves on the shore, and I am Queen of the blue salt road, and my story is only beginning.

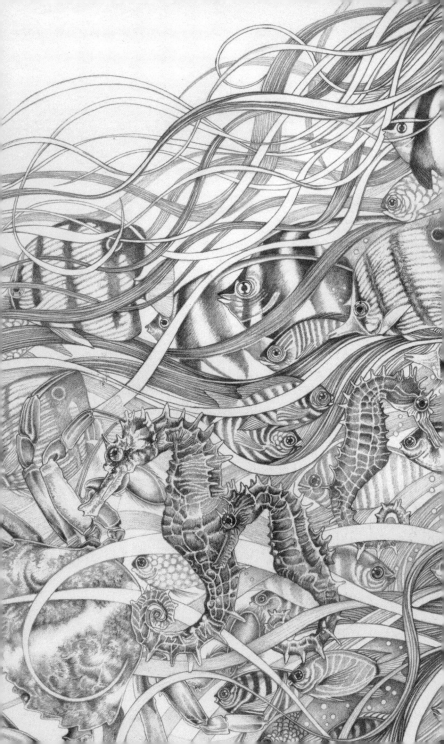